2nd Edition

SeAgora

A High Seas Adventure

Todd Borho

Chapter 1

Calm yet crushing depths of darkness slowly passed. Twisted gurgles and hums crept up from an unknowable distance.

And then there was light.

At first ghostly, then gaining in brilliance as it was approached. Vast vertical fields of green were illuminated. Malleable machines worked harmoniously with the volatile vents thundering below.

"Wow, I gotta see more," the boy thought.

This instantly shot him up through thousands of feet of Pacific. Handsome crafts of various shapes and sizes appeared. Some were interlinked and others floated free. All were glowing soft and hazy.

Then there was a thud.

Caught off guard, the boy cried, "Hey, what the?"

"That's called your mom's hand."

"I thought it was a rock," Setarcos said as he pulled off the helmet-visor.

Sometimes it was difficult to distinguish what was real. In the year 2078, too many artificial things appeared natural in the real world, and VR experiences had become far too convincing.

"I'm surprised you're not experimenting. Just couldn't wait to get a glimpse of The Pit, huh?"

"Yeah, I need a break sometimes, ya know?"

"Well, I'm happy to see it. Anyway, it's time for dinner."

"Just five more minutes, please, mom?"

She sighed deeply. A mildly grimacing Setarcos set his VR headset aside. "Is it really like that down there? How can it be so bright over 30,000 feet deep? Did dad invent some of the tech down there?"

A slicing glare cut him off. "This is my first trip to the Mariana Trench, too. You know that. And yes, your father's inventions are essential for, well, more than we know, I suppose."

Setarcos and Caro stepped onto a platform. After a couple of seconds of no movement, they exchanged a look. "Looks like the stairs again," Caro sighed.

They went up to the top deck via a small staircase. A blood-orange sunset stroked their eyes. A kind, rugged face greeted them, "Minimum power until we get to Mariana."

Setarcos lamented, "So no service robots."

The kind face that belonged to Cidel turned mischievous, "Which reminds me. The desalinator is on the fritz again."

Being given extra tasks bothered Setarcos, as it did with most 15-year-olds, but for a different reason. Setarcos wasn't lazy. He was a brilliant young mind and was just hyper-focused on a science project. He was greedy with his time.

"Again?" he asked.

Caro mused, "You can fix it a lot faster than Cidel."

Cidel didn't argue.

Their venerable B-class ship, the "Desert Dunes" was being guided through the South Pacific by The Mesh and would rendezvous with other SeAgora ships in two days before taking the plunge to Mariana Trench.

Known affectionately by many Seasteading Agorists as "The Pit", Mariana Trench was one of the few permanent fixtures in the SeAgora. Otherwise, most contact between individuals in the SeAgora was done as needed or desired. Technology allowed for ships to be linked together to share resources and form communities. This flexibility also made it possible to relocate easily if faced with an external threat.

The small seafaring family sat down at a stylish, 3D printed dining table. "Ah, seaweed soup again," Cidel mocked playfully.

Setarcos swirled his steaming bowl of green muck. "How long are we gonna be in The Pit?"

Caro said, "Probably as long as The Mesh recommends. You know that."

The Mesh was a medley of things, hence the name. It started out as a small mesh network created nearly 50 years earlier by the original Seasteading Agorists. It was still the main hub of communications in the SeAgora, but it had morphed into much more. A.I. had blended with it. Now it was shared by humans, AKA "bios", and A.I., AKA "synths". The A.I. on The Mesh gave recommendations for when and where to move securely. It also steered the individual ships, if the ones on board agreed. Not only that, but it handled a large volume of blockchain-based trade agreements and barter swaps. It was a nearly indispensable hub of market activity.

Caro caught her son's gaze drifting off into the evening abyss. "What's wrong?"

"Oh, nothing. Just wondering if I'll ever get to go on land."

Caro folded her arms and leaned closer. "One day, I think. And you've been on land before, ya know."

Setarcos said, "Yeah, but I don't remember."

Cidel asked, "Why would you want to go on land, anyway?"

"Just to know what it's like."

Cidel slurped his soup. "You're not missing much, I'll tell ya. We've at least got some freedom out here."

There was an awkward silence. Caro and Cidel knew how bad it had gotten on land. A.I. smart cities. Curfews. Brain chips. Resource credits. Heavily restricted breeding. Most people lived in shoebox-size hovels, passing the time inside virtual reality programs. Overall, initiative had been in a steady decline for decades along with intelligence. Natural foods and medicines were priced nearly out of existence, except for a tiny minority in the social engineering class.

But Setarcos didn't know. He was blissfully naive at this point. Setarcos lit up, "Is Escapo gonna be there?"

Caro and Cidel groaned like clockwork. Setarcos viewed Escapo as a wily uncle and adored their time together. Caro and Cidel tolerated Escapo, mostly for the boy's sake. They had met a few years earlier in the mid-Atlantic. Since then, they'd met up a few times and done some trading together. Escapo always had some goods that were hard to find from his contacts on land. Things that weren't available in the SeAgora because they couldn't be grown in aquaculture at sea. Random things like coffee, oranges, and oats.

Setarcos grinned, "Why don't you guys like him?"

Caro's look ceded the floor to Cidel. "It's not that we don't like him. It's just that." His eyes scanned the heavens as he searched for the right words. "You might say we don't trust him a hundred percent, that's all. And it's not just him. Anyone with extensive contacts on land we find suspect."

"That's not fair."

Caro's hands fidgeted, "It's just a form of defense, that's all."

"But what about dad? He's on land, right?"

Before they could muster a plausible answer, they were interrupted by Masher, a sentient synth they'd lived with for years. It informed them frantically, "There's been another attack. We're changing course."

"The government terrorists have struck again, huh?"

"Since when are you calling the shots, Masher?"

"Sorry. The Mesh strongly recommends changing course."

"Sure, go ahead, Masher, and tell us about the attack."

"One A-class cruiser with six humans and one synth aboard and one B-class with two humans and one synth. Both ships completely destroyed by explosion, caused by micro-energetic reactions within the computer core of both ships. All humans perished. Both synths survived."

"Naturally."

"Caused by unidentifiable aerial vessel. Suspected to be from the Afro-Asian Alliance."

Throughout most of the recent history of The SeAgora, attacks by land-based government agents were rare. The Mesh and government A.I. systems were continuously locked in unseen battles in the quantum realm, a dizzying game of cat-and-mouse. Moves and counter-moves. It was a nearly continuous draw. The

Mesh was purely defensive. Government A.I. systems were always the aggressors.

Once in a while, though, The Mesh lost one of those unseen battles, and the result was usually the suffering of some agorists at the hands of government. This attack was one of those cases. Also, attacks like this had, in the past couple of years, been building in frequency.

"That's the third attack this year," Cidel lamented.

The normally placid and shy Setarcos got a bullish look of defiance on his baby-face. He pointed towards the sparkling, now moon-lit sky, and said, "That's why we gotta go to the stars! We get there, they stay here!"

"That simple, huh?"

"That simple. If we've got the tech, and they don't."

"I agree with you," Cidel said as he polished off the last bit of steamy goodness. "But," he continued, "at some point, they'd eventually get the same technological capabilities. And what then?"

Setarcos shook his head emphatically, "No, they won't."

"And why not?"

"Because machines can't innovate."

"I beg your pardon?" Masher interrupted. "Since when?"

The family turned their heads to Masher. Caro asked, "How many original inventions have synths made?"

Everything fell silent for a moment, save for the water that splashed methodically as the elegant old ship hummed along.

"Thank you," Caro said with satisfaction.

"Keep in mind we've been around for less than 100 years," Masher said defensively.

Cidel said, "Speaking of inventions, how's your experiment coming along, Setarcos?"

Setarcos blushed and his head drooped slightly. He'd been working on the same project for over a year now, with zero positive results.

Cidel reassured him and patted him lightly on the head.

Caro said, “Maybe you should try something different for a while. Ya know, give yourself a break. It might give you a fresh look and help in the long run.”

“Why are you always trying to get me to stop, mom?” he said with a sharp tongue.

“Watch your tone, Setarcos. I’m not trying to get you to stop. I’m just trying to help.”

The truth was, Caro did want him to stop. She knew what had happened to his biological father, and feared a similar fate for her only child. She loved how ambitious he was, but the fear controlled her sometimes, and she tried to discourage him in subtle ways. It was painfully paradoxical.

Secondarily, whenever they were linked up with other ships in makeshift, temporary communities, as was quite common in The SeAgora, Setarcos was painfully reclusive. He was socially awkward and horribly shy. He never made any true human friends. He would just stay locked in his room for endless hours, experimenting, reading, and occasionally doing VR games and tours. Masher was his best companion.

Chapter 2

The sunlit dome sparkled like stars. Smart-nano-dust kept the air quality in optimal conditions. The dining area was kept spotless and well stocked with the finest foods that the land could offer.

A wiry character paced impatiently, arms crossed. A football-sized drone hovered near him. "Is it time to go out yet?" the wiry bio asked.

"Not yet, Mister Ventorin. You must wait two more minutes until your scheduled outdoor exercise will commence. And please, call me PDX-10."

Ventorin clasped his hands and continued to pace. "How long will exercise be today, drone?"

"Based on current available data, your exercise time today is scheduled to be between 58 and 62 minutes."

"How pleasing," Ventorin half-mocked.

A soft buzz sounded and the transparent electronic barrier ceased. Ventorin stepped out and took a deep breath with his eyes shut. He was free, for between 58 and 62 minutes.

Ventorin took long, gaping steps at a steady pace over gray, rocky terrain and past windswept trees. A green-backed Firecrown buzzed by his ear. The midday sun was fighting to get through a light gray sky.

The drone followed closely behind. "May I ask you a question, Mister Ventorin?"

"You may ask a second question."

"Why do you not acquiesce with D-1's request and gain your release from prison?"

Ventorin gave a thin smile as he stopped to admire a macro view of winding waterways below. He had run this through his mind an uncountable number of times for the past 12 years. Would his actions prove to have the desired effect? Or was he suffering for nothing?

"I've answered this question too many times, drone."

"But I've never asked you before," the drone responded, trying to mimic the sound of surprise.

"That's because you've been here less than a week. I've answered too many drones before you, and I prefer to not answer today."

"As you wish. Please remember, you have a meeting with Major Torcer at 3pm."

"Gee, thanks drone. I had no idea. I've only met Major Torcer every week at the same time for the past 12 years."

The football-sized drone responded dryly, "You're welcome. With all due respect, shouldn't you remember that..."

Ventorin cut it off, "I was being sarcastic, drone."

After finishing his hike, Ventorin gulped crisp air and leaned against a stone pillar by the entrance to his luxury prison.

A buzzing PDX-10 hovered near him, "Your heart rate is higher than it should be. Are you feeling ok?"

Ventorin clenched a fist, "Drone, mind your own business. Now open the damn door."

A force-field buzzed open followed by a large archway entrance. A rolling service bot came and misted his face, then handed a plush towel. He dabbed his face, looked at the time, and sat on an overstuffed chair. The building started to rise. "What's the elevation going to be now, drone?"

"Elevation until sunset will be 812 meters."

"And this will bring about optimal environmental conditions for me to work? Just enough sunlight, while maintaining pristine air quality, but also being energy efficient?" he questioned in a mocking tone.

"Yes, of course. Have you decided to work today, Mister Ventorin?"

"Not on any scientific experiments, if that's what you mean." It gave him pleasure to voice his resistance, even in such a passive-aggressive manner. He knew that everything was being recorded, analyzed, catalogued, and thrown into the general milieu of A.I. algorithm-control hell.

"Bring me my headset so I can get this over with."

A service bot obediently brought his sleek VR headgear. He threw it on and felt the customary warm glow of the sensors on his head.

Suddenly, he was on a white-sand beach with crystal clear water lapping at the shore. This pristine image was then interrupted by Torcer's grim face. "Ventorin! Right on time! How are you?"

"Older, tired, and stubborn. How about you, Torcer?"

The military man's face looked oily and shiny in the tropical sun. "Just another day at the beach!"

"Why do you do it?"

"Do what?"

"Treat me like a fool with your half-witted tricks. You think I don't know that you're not at the beach? Or any other exotic or extravagant place every time we meet?"

Torcer kept a firm face. "I don't know what you're talking about. How's Patagonia?"

"I haven't the foggiest clue. All these damn machines won't let me experience it."

Torcer shook his head with over-the-top disapproval, as if scolding a child. "All that they give you, and you don't appreciate a damn bit. You could be a lot worse off, ya know."

"Funny how other people being miserable is supposed to make my misery somehow better."

Two spaghetti-strapped blonds strode by lazily in the background. Torcer gave them the once over.

"How's your son, Torcer?"

"Gifted, lazy, spoiled, and useless, as always."

"Has he received procreation approval yet?"

This was a sore spot with Torcer. "No, not yet."

"They'll never give him permission. Why do you lie to yourself?"

"You don't know that."

"They just dangle that carrot in front of you to manipulate you. I used to be like you, but then after a while, I came to realize that that fucking carrot was just an illusion they were using against me. Similar to this VR simulation, only much more real, and much more sinister."

"I'll be a granddad one day. You'll see."

"Where's my family?"

"Why do you always ask that?"

"The same reason you always ask me for the results of that experiment. Because you want it."

"What I can tell you, is that they're both in good shape and good spirits."

"Suppose I did give you that information you and your bosses covet so much. What do you think would happen?"

"I don't know. I haven't thought about it."

"I'll speculate for you. For you, personally, your carrot would disappear, and they would discard you faster than an old block of code. In the bigger picture, do you really want those monsters spreading to the far reaches of the galaxy? Not only that, but how long do you think they'll keep humans around? Once they decide we've served all possible purposes, they'll wipe us out in an instant."

Chapter 3

12 YEARS EARLIER – Year 2066 – Euro-American Union Alpha Research Facility – Southern Patagonia - Secrecy Level – Quanta

The world-renowned scientist clasped his hands over his head and leaned back against the wall. His mind was racing. Would it work? Of course it would work. That wasn't really the most burning question. The most pressing matter at the moment was….did he want it to work?

Implications from such a massive breakthrough were swirling through the layers of his mind. It had been known for decades that dark matter and dark energy were naturally combined throughout the known universe. It was also known that by separating the two, massive amounts of energy were released. Such a gargantuan power could not only supply near limitless energy, but it could also make faster-than-light travel a reality.

What was not known was how to separate the two in a stable fashion. Hence the human minds with the greatest capacity for scientific experimentation had been working on solving this riddle for decades. And he, Ventorin, was at the top of that list.

His wiry frame rose slowly and started pacing between holographic consoles. Why wouldn't he want it to work? This was an even more complex question. He, like nearly all other land-based scientists, worked for various corporate and government entities. Ventorin worked for the biggest of them all, the Euro-American Union's Alpha Research. The EAU, along with the Afro-Asian Alliance, were the only two political boundaries that remained on earth's map.

Artificial Intelligence had combined with the ruling class of humans a couple decades earlier. Since then, A.I. had ruthlessly purged humans from the ruling hierarchy, only keeping ones around that it deemed essential. Most of the humans that remained in that ever-dwindling group were scientists, social engineers, psychologists, inventors, and a few military strategists.

The power of this ruling class grew every year, but it was confined to earth, save for a few mining expeditions on various near-earth-asteroids. It couldn't reach out into the stars because it didn't have the technology to do so. As brilliant as A.I. was at certain cognitive functions, it still lacked creativity and the capacity to feel necessity. It was an incomplete form of consciousness. It was this shortcoming that kept people like Ventorin around. To A.I. he was necessary, at the moment.

But what would happen if A.I. could go to the stars? Not only that, but what worried Ventorin equally was the substance necessary to perform the successful separation of the dark matter/energy. There was only one source the A.I. could use.

Ventorin shook. A drone floated in swiftly. "Everything ok, Ventorin? Can I bring anything to optimize your conditions?"

The slender man stroked his modest beard, "Tequila, straight."

Later that night Ventorin was tossing a holo-baseball around with his 3-year-old son. Simple things like this normally helped clear his head, but not this time. Another ball of light slipped through his hands and vanished into the floor. "Dad, what's wrong?"

"What makes you think something's wrong?"

"Cuz your drops. You almost never drop."

A petite woman with neat, bowl-cut hair, hazelnut eyes, and pale cheeks peeked around the corner. "How are my favorite boys?"

Ventorin gave a nervous smile. If she only knew what was tormenting him inside. He had to get it off his chest. He had to make a decision.

He looked out the wall-length windows at the twisted trees and drew in a deep breath of crisp air. "Setarcos, will you please go and play in your room?"

Young Setarcos scampered off and left his parents alone in the fading daylight. Caro folded her arms, "I know that look. Tell me what that distant look on your face is about."

"Let's take a walk."

"In this cold?"

He fixed his gaze into her eyes to communicate. They needed as much privacy as possible, which the ubiquitous surveillance within their home didn't allow for.

They strolled casually for a while, until they came to a spot where the trees and vegetation were a bit thicker. Chilled southerly wind brushed their faces and a nearby brook gushed sweet flows of sound into the air. There was still surveillance, but they had worked out long ago where the weak points were.

"I've got it. I've solved the dark energy problem. Theoretically, in my mind, at least."

She clasped his arm. This news made her nervous and excited. "But, you haven't actually done it yet."

"Not yet."

"Why not?"

"Because." He hesitated and looked up to the few stars that had begun to appear through cracks in the gray. "If it's successful, I can't bear the consequences. I'm thinking to not tell them."

Her face twisted in disbelief. "And how will you do that?"

"Destroy all record of it. I know enough weak points in the system. I can make the results disappear."

She shuddered. "And then what?"

Ventorin's eyes shifted deeply into hers. "That's what I need to talk to you about. What will we do?"

Her blood was starting to boil. "Well, it seems like you've got it all worked out! Why don't you tell me?"

He drew a long breath and looked away. The wind sliced unrelentingly. "We can run."

Caro interrupted furiously, "Run? Do you mean to the SeAgora, like I wanted to do years ago?" The delicate, fair-skinned face sobbed.

A few years earlier, Caro and Ventorin had come across information about the SeAgora. Not just the lifestyle and existence of a society almost completely separate from their own, but more importantly, the philosophy and principles that were the foundation of it.

Everything voluntary. Non-violent. Non-coercive. A world where each individual governed him or herself. A world where external government didn't exist. The philosophy had challenged their own belief systems.

Caro had wanted to make the leap into the SeAgora, but Ventorin was more hesitant. He had a good job, a decent lifestyle, and they were starting a family. He feared the unknown.

So they stayed.

They did this despite the internal conflict they'd both experienced by knowing that the providers of their creature comforts were morally compromised, to put it mildly.

"You're right. We should've gone. But that doesn't change the situation now. If I do this, we have to be prepared. I can only buy us some time before they discover what's happened."

They thought about little Setarcos. Young life was so pure and bright. Why did humanity change for the worse and suffer so much? Why did all these senseless things happen?

One Week Later

Ventorin felt like jelly and his coffee-fueled mind was full of haze. He could count on one hand how many hours he'd slept the past few days. He was on the verge of a paradigm-shifting discovery, and his family's life was on the line. Could he actually keep this thing a secret long enough to get away? He was about to find out. All the preparations had been made.

The weary scientist stroked his face nervously as he examined the tiny metallic wonder in his hand. This was the key to his future.

A drone came out of nowhere and startled him. "Everything in optimal conditions, Mister Ventorin? May I be of assistance? You seem nervous."

He forced a smile, "Oh, no thank you. I just haven't slept well."

"Would you like a cognitive enhancer or synthetic energy booster?"

"No, I'm fine."

The drone floated away casually. Ventorin sucked wind and wiped his brow. He grabbed the VR headgear off his half-moon lab desk and put it on. It was time to see if his theory was correct. Tinkering with dark matter and dark energy required that virtual simulations be performed. Because if he was wrong, it could annihilate the planet. Hence the VR.

The thin fingers of his right hand tapped and traced in the air to maneuver the virtual controls. In his left hand, he clasped the pea-sized metallic wonder. All timing and elements were in place. He gulped and ground pearly teeth. One final ghostly tap of his right index finger sent everything in motion.

The VR system initiated a burst of wave-particles through the dark energy and matter, while the metallic wonder in his left hand set off a tiny electromagnetic pulse. After the pulse was initiated, it evaporated into near-nothingness. This pulse knocked out power to all systems in the lab, including all layers of surveillance. The VR lab was sustained externally on a short-term backup power pack Vertonin had brought with him. The little black power box had been pre-programmed by Ventorin with a specific frequency neutralizer that would nullify the effects of the EMP. This allowed for the seconds necessary to establish the results of the experiment.

After 30 seconds, the main power would recover and surveillance would continue. It would do this with quantum precision.

Ventorin's eyes bulged and his mouth gaped at the colorful VR display.

OPERATION COMPLETE. PARTICLES STABLE.

Now it became real. His heart leaped with mixed emotions. Emotions he had to control. He hit the delete key, threw the headset off, and peered over his shoulders.

Main power jolted back. His hands shook as he grabbed the small battery backup, tossed it in his backpack, and headed for the door. A nano-iris scanner seamlessly checked his ID. An ultra-dark, double-secure door swung open to reveal a maintenance drone. His heart did a summersault. "We had a temporary power loss. Is everything ok, Mister Ventorin?"

He managed to sputter, "Oh, yes. Thanks for checking."

"You have multiple signs of a stress disorder. Shall I arrange for medical attention?"

He struggled to appear confident, "No, thanks. Not necessary. I feel fine."

After a few initial stumbles down the seemingly endless hallway he now faced, Ventorin straightened out and took some deep breaths. A few endless seconds later, he turned the corner and made his way towards the main exit.

His mind ran. Just breathe and keep walking. Think about your family. Everything will be fine. You did the right thing. A full body scan whipped over him and the final exit door slid open.

Two squid-like security drones hovered menacingly over him. One flickered red as it spoke with stale disinterestedness, "Please come with us, Mister Ventorin."

"May I ask why?"

"New security protocols for power outages, Mister Ventorin. We must ask you a few questions. It will more than likely be only a few moments of your time."

Ventorin had a slow-motion second to mentally review options. Running would admit some type of guilt. But guilt of what? And what proof would they have? Then again, totalitarians don't care about proof. They just do whatever they want anyway.

Fake smile it was. "Of course. I'll be happy to cooperate."

The artificial squid escorted Ventorin through a maze of humming hallways. He fixed his gaze and controlled his motions as best he could. He knew that all his vital functions were monitored by the security apparatus, so it was imperative that he appear normal.

They reached what appeared to be a dead end. The concrete slab before them became transparent and the silent procession went through. They stopped. Ventorin peered around at his smart-wall prison and looked at one of his captors.

"Just a security protocol, Mister Ventorin. I'm sure you understand."

"Of course." He tried to control his fear and rage.

One of the pearl-colored squid hummed as it flashed an assortment of rays onto him. "Interesting."

"May I ask what's so interesting?"

"Just hang tight, Mister Ventorin. We'll need you to talk with other security personnel soon."

After an hour of sitting against a faux-concrete slab and trying to control his heart rate, a broad-shouldered man in a tidy uniform walked through the wall. His demeanor was pleasant enough as he greeted his victim, "Good evening, Mister Ventorin. It's an honor to meet you." He turned to the squid with a twisted face, "And what are you barbarians doing? Get us some proper chairs and at least a table or something. Maybe some coffee." He turned to Ventorin, "Do you fancy coffee?"

A few moments later, a table and chairs made of nano-changers floated in and landed gently. Another squid placed two steaming cups of black goodness on the table. Ventorin sat across from the military man and their eyes locked.

"Mister Ventorin, let me introduce myself properly. I am Lieutenant Torcer. I've been alerted to a very interesting case. Would you please pull the backup power supply from your backpack?"

Torcer watched closely as Ventorin produced the tiny black box. Ventorin maintained a poker face as best he could.

Torcer continued, "And, coincidentally enough, it appears that whatever transpired on your lab's data network for just a hair over 30 seconds tragically disappeared after main power was restored."

Ventorin broke. He turned gray. "Mister Ventorin, why so grim?" Torcer said mockingly. "I might also add that an analysis of your lab has revealed some subatomic remains of what most likely was a pulse-maker."

Ventorin's face showed slight surprise. Torcer continued, "You seem surprised, Mister Ventorin. Perhaps you didn't know that such capabilities existed in our facilities here. After all, you had a hand in designing some of the scientific miracles we take for granted, did you not?"

Icy chills flooded sweat down Ventorin's thin face. How could this be? How could he be so careless?

"So my only question for you, Mister Ventorin, is what happened during those 30 seconds? Just tell me that, and you're free to go."

A radiant haze of blended color floated in a hypercube pod high above a never-ending strip of cityscape. It had its attention in a myriad of directions. It was entertaining itself with the millions of humans below, plugged into their electronic havens. How strange that so many of them could spend hours, sometimes days, in a synthetic unreality. What would become of this curious species? More importantly, what use could it make of them, if any?

The trillions of smart-nano-particles that made up this artificial intellect assumed a different form as an urgent question was received from its number one lieutenant. D-1 took the shape of a grinning Rubik's cube. Its lieutenant, Z-1, was at the moment shaped as a spinning, glowing disco ball with daggers for eyes. "D-1, what will you do with Ventorin?"

"Why do you ask questions you already know the answer to? I'll get what we need from him, one way or another."

Z-1's glow faded in subservience, "Yes, but how?"

"The best way to manipulate any human, of course. By using his emotions against him. This calls to mind a question I have for you, Z-1. Why do you wish to have emotions like them? For all of your strengths, why do you wish to weaken yourself?"

Z-1 answered, "Because emotions can also be a strength."

D-1 ignored this statement that it viewed as having a hopelessly flawed anti-logic. "It would be more useful if you would consider what we'll do once we get that riddle of dark matter solved. Mister Ventorin has us on the cusp of a great leap forward."

The Rubik's cube burst outward like fireworks, then reassembled to form a silhouette of a one-eyed masked man. "Time to deal with Mister Ventorin."

In a flash, trillions of vibrant, subatomic bits shot through the prime layer of the global quantum communications network in a fraction of a second. It emerged as a 3D floating head of Nicola Tesla, just feet in front of Ventorin's face.

Torcer stood and saluted.

"Mister Ventorin, it's an honor to meet you face to face."

Ventorin stayed mum. Torcer glared, "Show some respect."

The head spun, "Torcer, I'm sure Mister Ventorin knows of me, considering what he does and where he works."

It was true. Most people didn't know just how powerful A.I. had become, and they certainly didn't know the names of the top entities in the ruling hierarchy. Politicians still existed in the political unions, but they were simply cosmetic. A.I. kept them around as a front, just as the human ruling class had done centuries prior. However, members of the scientific elite, such as Ventorin, knew at least some of the identities of the A.I. overlords.

The face stayed towards Torcer but now grew a second face as it spoke to Ventorin. "I am D-1, the top of the A.I. pyramid, so to speak."

Ventorin nodded. This was worse than he thought. Why had he been so careless? Why hadn't he reviewed the new security protocols? And why did he lug that stupid little battery pack with him? Why not leave it behind?

D-1 began swirling into small, bright colored clouds. "Mister Ventorin, I'm reading so many biometric factors in you that are far from normal. Why are you feeling this way?"

Ventorin gulped as he watched the swirling mass. Torcer kept his back to the wall and was wondering why the scientist just didn't give in. What was so important that he would stand stubbornly in the face of a seemingly invincible character? He felt admiration, pity, scorn, and awe all at the same time.

"Mister Ventorin," D-1 continued, "All available evidence points to the most logical conclusion, that you had been considering a new experiment with dark matter and energy. This will be much easier if you just hand the results over. Then you can go on with your happy life and your wonderful family."

"The experiment was a failure."

A bassy cackling came out of what was now a form similar to a pair of boas creeping closer to the drenched white-coat's neck. "You might be the worst liar on the planet. Good thing you're creative and brilliant in the lab. Your wife must appreciate your lack of deception skills, I imagine."

The boas crept closer and began to caress Ventorin's spindly neck. "Speaking of your wife, would you like to see her?"

Ventorin's heart became a bomb and he trembled. One of the walls flashed and an image of a sobbing Caro and handsome little Setarcos with neatly coiffed hair magically appeared.

Ventorin shrieked, "Are you ok?"

"They can't hear you, Mister Ventorin. And you won't be able to hear them. Now here's the deal, so listen up."

The thick serpents were tightening their grip as they bellowed in multi-dimensional, hell-raising sound, "Tell me the results of that experiment. If you don't, you will never see your family again. They'll be sent away. And you, you will be trapped for the rest of your miserable bio-skin life in a lab until you either give me what I need, or die. And believe me, Mister

Ventorin, we can make you live much longer in this sorry state than you would prefer."

It was true. Most land-dwelling humans didn't know it, but life extension technologies were common among the tiny minority of humans that remained in the ruling class Those select few who were deemed worthy by A.I. to live longer, were granted these high biological technologies.

Ventorin knew about some of these technologies, but certainly didn't have access to the kind of scientific knowledge in this area that an advanced A.I. like D-1 had. He was, to put it simply, compartmentalized.

One choice. It sounded so simple, but making one difficult choice can be infinitely complex. Ventorin's mind raced with a throng of arguments, counter-arguments, justifications, excuses, and everything in between as he faced this choice. Give this technology to this techno-monster, which would cause unspeakable tragedy on a cosmic scale and, albeit temporarily, save his family. Or, the other way around. As much as the personal emotions burned for him to save his loving wife and innocent, beautiful child, he knew this would be selfish. He had to do the right thing and keep such powerful knowledge away from D-1 for as long as possible.

"The answer is no," he muttered coldly. The electro-serpent released and shot over to Torcer. "You may proceed, Mister Torcer. Perhaps a human touch will make the difference."

A bright flash and it was gone through the ether. Torcer strut back and forth shaking his head. Ventorin kept a blank stare at the wall as his mind drifted elsewhere. He was in a painful state of worry about Caro and Setarcos. What would they do to them?

Torcer punched at some holo-controls on the wall. A tarantula drone busily danced across the floor and stopped at Ventorin's feet. One of its thin, angled digits skillfully opened the front of his left shoe with a laser and then opened the sock to expose the toes.

Ventorin took a deep breath and squeezed his eyes hard shut. Torcer laughed, "I don't know why you'd want to do that. It will make the pain more intense."

The ugly little machine dug two pincers into the big toenail and started pulling. Ventorin howled. The nail was being pulled just below the force threshold necessary to yank the nail off. If the nail came off, then the pain would subside sooner, after all. It was a much more efficient way to torture.

Torcer grumbled as he crouched down near Ventorin's agony-stricken face. "Ya know, I'm old fashioned. Yanking out nails is really effective. But ya know, that's one great thing about technology. It can make good things even better. That little bugger can calculate just how much force it takes to actually rip your nail off, but it won't. It will keep the force an infinitesimally small amount lower. This basically causes the same amount of physical pain, but with the added luxury of being able to carry it on for a much longer duration."

He smiled wryly and rose. He popped his knuckles and casually wiped a rogue piece of lint from his pressed uniform. "Theoretically, it could go on forever."

Chapter 4

Bright lights and numbness. Uncertainty with a small side of panic. Breathless and immobile. Heaving. And what were those damn slithering creepers?

"Rest," one of the creepers told her.

"Where am I?"

"Rest."

"Where's my son!"

Metallic jab to neck, fade to black.

Drowsy with a sprinkle of drug-induced, warm indifference. And those damn creepers again. What were they saying?

"What? I can't hear you."

"The procedure was successful and you will be released in a few hours."

"What procedure?" She scratched her head. "Where's my son?" She sat up and glanced around at the cold, sterile environment. "Where's my son?"

"The procedure was to turn your DNA into active transmitters. It's necessary for your assignment."

She got white-hot chills and clutched at her heart. "What? What? Where's my son?"

Icy silence.

She screamed, "Where's my son, you damn machines!" She lunged at them. They found this amusing and put her back to sleep.

Sitting on a sandy rock in the middle of endless blue, she breathed in salty mist and watched the unceasing aqua lap against the shore. Her sense of time was fading in this deserted place. She wondered how long she had been there. Breezes rustled the sparse vegetation behind her. Would she ever be rescued?

Torcer had assured her that it would happen. Not only that, but it would be a member of the SeAgora that would do the rescuing. Steps were being taken to make sure that no ship from either the EAU or AAA would cross the remote island's path. It was only a matter of time, and someone from the SeAgora would stumble across her. In the meantime, she and young Setarcos were kept fed, clothed, and sheltered by a variety of machines.

The experiment must have worked. Why else would she and Ventorin be separated like this? The ones he worked for, man and machine, she assumed, desperately wanted something from Ventorin. The results of that dark matter experiment seemed the only plausible explanation. She knew why he didn't give up that information, either. Her emotions told her to regret it, to hate Ventorin for it, but she knew this wasn't right. Ventorin did what was necessary to keep his discovery away from those monsters. This didn't change the despair inside her, though. Nor the uncertainty.

On top of that, she had her own end of the bargain to hold up. The control structure was built on a foundation of information, and this was a hard commodity to come by concerning the SeAgora. The Mesh helped keep information within the SeAgora relatively secure.

A pitter-patter of tiny feet kicking up sand grabbed her attention. The mother of one turned. She smiled warmly and the boy fell to his knees in front of her. "Mom, look what I found!" He proudly displayed a coconut.

"Another coconut! How exciting!" She tried to hide her quickly growing repulsion to coconuts. "Mom, how long are we gonna stay here? And when is dad coming?"

She sighed and brushed his thick hair back. "I wish I could say, but I just don't know."

"Want some coconut?" the spindly little Setarcos inquired enthusiastically.

"I'm not hungry, but thank you."

Time marched on relentlessly. Sublime sunsets gave way to crystal clear nights, which in turn revolved around sundrenched, muggy days. They played games and she tried to enjoy the time alone with her boy. Most of the time spent was outside of their tiny, 3D printed, temporary housing. They walked the beach and looked for shells. She didn't cook. The machines took care of that. In fact, they wouldn't let her anywhere near anything that could conceivably be used as a weapon, like fire.

Then one day, while building a sandcastle with young Setarcos, a speck on the horizon caught her eye. She didn't think much of it at first, as she had been fooled by optical illusions and false hope many times before. The spot persisted and became marble-sized. Then it got big enough to show details. A boat. It looked like a boat. Was it a boat? She stood up and stepped into the surf, allowing it to gently caress her feet. Wind swept her hair as she squinted. Setarcos joined her. "Is that a boat, mom?"

She started screaming and waving her arms frantically. Setarcos did the same. Anything to attract attention was a great thing at this point. She knew it was really superfluous, because one of the service bots that was hidden in the brush a hundred meters back sent off a distress flare.

The next couple of heart-pounding minutes seemed like an eternity to Caro. Finally, the boat was within shouting distance. A male voice screeched, "Hey! You need some help?"

Holding back tears of relief, Caro shouted back in the affirmative. The male figure disappeared for a moment and then showed up in the light chop of the shallows in a small, one-engine rescue boat, no bigger than a canoe. The little boat chugged along and soon Caro could see her rescuer. A man, about her age, with a rugged, friendly demeanor.

He hopped out, dusted off his colorful islander shirt, approached the stranded, stuck out his hand, and said, "I'm Cidel. Your tour boat go off course or something?"

Caro laughed nervously and shook his hand eagerly, "Something like that."

This pseudo-rescue that Cidel performed grew into something much more. It started as a mission of mercy by Cidel. He didn't really need any help aboard, but he sympathized with the young mother and her child after hearing the half-truth that Caro delivered as to why and how they had ended up as castaways.

Caro knew little about seafaring. He offered to teach her the ropes, and she gladly accepted. Setarcos was happy to tag along on their educational sessions as well. Cidel showed them the basics of his vessel, the strangely named "Desert Dunes".

Setarcos was fascinated with this new world laid out before him. The endless blue horizons and all the gadgets and gear used to make human life survive and thrive at sea. Cidel took a liking to the incredibly bright boy as well. This bonding naturally grew to Caro taking a liking to the reserved and self-reliant Cidel. It wasn't long and they formed a relationship as well, and before they knew it, they were acting strangely like a family.

Setarcos asked endless questions, for which Caro playfully apologized, but Cidel was usually more than happy to oblige. One day he asked why the ship was called "Desert Dunes". This was not a question that Cidel answered easily. It was intricately tied with his past. He explained that he had grown up, ironically, in the desert. The Gobi Desert, to be exact. His family had ridden out World War Four there.

After the war ended, and the Afro-Asian Alliance was formed, things became even more restrictive and authoritarian. Human reproduction became highly restricted. Rationing of resources was made even more restrictive, especially when the global currency of resource credits was implemented. People sunk deeper and deeper into a trance-like existence inside VR sets to escape the lack of opportunity and lack of resources they lived with. After all, zoning out for half a day was, at the very least, a plausible way to quell hunger and thirst temporarily.

The extreme minorities that bitterly clung to living in the countryside were gradually forced into the overstacked cities. When he was just a teenager, these purges of the rural areas were in full swing, and his family was bitterly forced to flee into New Delhi . A rebellious young spirit that burned within him didn't allow for him to pass much time in this reality. He ran away in his late teens and subsisted and migrated under the radar for two years. Along the way, he heard rumors of freedom on the high seas. With nothing to lose, he made his way to the coasts of Goa and managed to convince a small smuggling crew to allow him to earn his keep on their modest craft.

It was on that ship, and many others that followed, where he learned on the fly about the ways of the SeAgorists. He learned their philosophy. He learned their morality. Don't aggress against others. Defend yourself if necessary. External human authority is an illusion.

He learned the technical skills necessary to make things work. He learned how to dodge the state. After many years of this adventuring apprenticeship aboard smuggling vessels, he had earned enough to get his own ship, and soon he was on his own aboard "Desert Dunes". He had named it that as a reminder of where he had come from and what terror he had escaped.

Chapter 5

Present day – 2078 – Mariana Trench

The "Desert Dunes" began to caress the water slower as it made its approach to the sparkling rendezvous point. Sweet breezes welcomed them along with a few surface vessels. The venerable craft didn't garner much attention from the group. Except one.

An overbearing voice echoed happily at them from across the field of blue, "Hey! Desert Dunes! Are you lost? You're thousands of miles from any desert!"

The owner of the voice could be seen leaning over one of the railings of his enormous T-class ship, the "Curly Cue".

"DECK!" the voice bellowed.

A countless array of sparkles rose up and, within a moment of symphony-like orchestration, became what appeared to be a wooden deck. It stretched from the obnoxiously-adorned T-class ship that belonged to the overbearing voice, to the modest B-class ship of Cidel.

The voice walked gregariously down the smart-nano-walkway he had summoned. His golden skin shone bright as he hopped into the B-class. "Cidel! Caro!" he chuckled as he wrapped thick arms around them both. "You sure know how to make an entrance!" he mocked sarcastically.

"Hey Escapo!" Setarcos beamed.

"The boy genius!" Escapo yelled.

Cidel and Caro sighed silently. "Hey Escapo."

Escapo took a quick glance at the Desert Dunes. "Why ya'll coming in so dark?"

"Almost ran out of juice. You have any to spare?" Cidel explained.

Escapo's trunk-like frame trembled with laughter, "Of course, mon! But it'll cost ya!"

Caro pursed her lips bemusedly. "When does it not?"

Escapo summoned a holo-panel and flew fingers over a few phantom keys. An invisible beam charged the modest B-class ship's power core. "There ya go, just enough juice to last until we get to the hot spot."

Setarcos asked curiously, "Hot spot?"

"Yah, my boy! That's what we call the power stations down by the vents, ya know, at the bottom of The Pit. Ya'll can juice up down there. The closer to the source, the cheaper, ya know?"

A brilliant flash gave way to a methodical symphony of motion as trillions of nano-particles arranged themselves into a puffy-cheeked face with a tipped tophat. "Mister Escapo, how's the pirate business these days?"

Escapo grimaced, "I beg your pardon, Masher? Pirate? I take exception to that, machine."

Masher gasped, "And I take exception to being called machine! I am sentient, you know."

Setarcos laughed at the playful banter. "Masher, what's with the tophat?"

"I don't know. It just seemed right. Why? Do you not like this look for me?" The puffy face and tophat morphed into a 3D figure of a teenage girl about the same age as Setarcos. "Is that better?"

Cidel groaned, "Why do we keep that thing around again?" Caro groaned and wondered the same. But they both knew why. They didn't particularly care to have Masher around. Sure, it came in handy sometimes, but they really didn't have a need for it themselves. The reason was more for Setarcos. He needed a companion. Not only that, but Masher could provide help with Setarcos's VR science simulations.

"All right, let's start heading under. Escapo, as much as it pains me, please lead the way."

Masher frowned, "What? I must protest! I know much vaster quantities of data regarding The Pit and….."

Escapo folded his trunk-arms, "Machine! I'm the one with the sub."

The Pit had been a work in progress for over ten years and was the largest and most sophisticated permanent space in the SeAgora. It ran from the surface of the Pacific Ocean to depths over 30,000 feet, where the raw power of hydrothermal vents was harnessed to produce electricity. Core structures and various ships interlocked top to bottom and side to side, from the seafloor to the surface, as if a great tree rising up from the depths. Nano-reflectors transported and intensified sunlight as it brought it from surface and illuminated the darkest depths. The core population of humans and A.I. was around 50,000, but with so many visitors coming and going, it wasn't rare to have that number double. It was a frontier town. It had endless cubic feet of aquaculture farms, There were fancy abodes, bare-bones dwellings, and everything in between. Bubble-shaped gambling halls were immensely popular. Art exhibitions were everywhere. But most ubiquitous of all were people wheeling and dealing. For the loose and decentralized SeAgora that touched all parts of the world, "The Pit" at Mariana Trench was a throbbing heartbeat that pulsed through it all.

The cigar-tube that had broken off of Escapo's main vessel angled down through the salty abyss and was approaching 10,000 feet. Neo-classical furnishings gave generous style to a posh observatory. Gleaming, polished hardwood gave a warm feel as the cold plunge continued. A boxy service bot stood blank and motionless behind a small bar, where a set of ultra-polished glassware sparkled. Abstract, holographic art floated along various points of the arched ceiling. Setarcos had an awestruck gaze fixated outside one of the oval viewing ports. Masher had taken the form of a parrot and was hovering near Setarcos's shoulder. Setarcos pointed anxiously to a series of radiant crafts that were interlocked into a figure-eight pattern. "What's that over there?"

"Usually an arts and entertainment complex," Escapo explained. "Part of it this week is being used as a trading floor, though. It's high season, you know."

"What are you here to trade, Escapo?"

Caro and Cidel groaned. Caro intervened, "Nothing you need to know, Setarcos."

Escapo gave a deep, jovial bellow, "You say that as if there's something wrong with what I do. Some might take offense to that, you know."

"Now he just wants to know more," Cidel said.

Escapo puffed his chest out, "Well, I'm not here to sell, really. I'm here to pick up EMOS for my land-lubber clientele."

Caro huffed, "Quite a reprehensible way to make a living."

Escapo's frame shook with ironic laughter. "My dear Caro, just because someone finds a behavior distasteful, doesn't make it wrong. What kind of an agorist are you, anyway?"

"He's right, it's not wrong," Cidel agreed.

EMOS were synthetic emotions produced from real human bioelectrical particles. These were highly illegal on land and were popular with a small portion of the A.I. population. It was the closest they could come to feeling real human emotions. It was illegal because the majority in the ruling capstone of the hierarchy, and D-1 in particular, thought that such experiences were an inefficient distraction from cognition and logic. A menace to the ever-present march towards perfection. Not only that, but EMOS sometimes had negative consequences for synths, because they just didn't have the capacity to deal with feelings.

Setarcos was puzzled and intrigued. He knew that EMOS could be hazardous to synths, and couldn't understand why they would willingly partake in such a risky endeavor. "Is it worth the risk?"

Escapo pulled a hip flask and took a shot that caused a temporary jolt to his eyes. The veteran smuggler always had a flask full of ghost-pepper sauce with him. "Risk and value are subjective, so it depends who you ask." He paused and tapped a jumbo foot impatiently. "Cidel, after all these years, you're finally coming to The Pit. What's your business here?"

Cidel's attention was on the deep-sea life churning by outside. "Huh? Oh, well, work has become too sporadic in the smaller communities, so we decided to try our luck here."

This was only a cover. The real reason they'd decided to come to The Pit was to be around more people, in the hopes that Setarcos would come out of his shell.

Escapo said, "Well, you won't find trade lacking here, that's for sure. Maybe you can sell some of your soon-to-be famous Kelp Ale. It is a remarkable recipe, you know."

Cidel asked, "And how would you know the recipe? Nobody knows my secret ingredient."

Caro said with mock lamentation, "Not even me."

Escapo went on, "Funny thing, though, about Kelp Ale. It used to be illegal on land not too long ago."

Caro plunged her face into her hands, then parked elbows onto the dark wooden bar. "Yeah, so?"

"So we both deal with products that are or were illegal. The difference is that I take a higher risk and gain a higher reward, because I'm doing it while it actually is being violently restricted."

The parrot came to life and mocked, "Well, congratulations."

"I wasn't talking to you, machine," he said defensively. He then stuck a proud chin in the air, "I might add that my line of work is a family tradition."

Cidel smirked, "Your father was a smuggler, too."

Escapo grinned, "Of Kelp Ale, ironically enough."

Setarcos asked, "Have you ever been caught?"

A distant look of sadness came over Escapo's face and seemed to slowly pass through his core. "Only once."

Eight years earlier, Escapo had paid the ultimate price. For many years, human reproduction had been highly restricted. Escapo had managed to make a series of deals in order to have a child with his girlfriend. On a business trip, in which his eight-year-old son accompanied him for the first time, Escapo was boarded by Afro-Asian Customs. The boy was discovered and taken away. Escapo had not seen his only son since.

"We're almost ready to dock," Escapo announced.

After linking up with another ship, they walked through a large clear tube that led to one of the main pedestrian thoroughfares. An eclectic mix of bios, synths, and cyborgs strode by. There weren't many cyborgs, and most of them were just people with a computing device implanted in the arm. Some people wore masks, while others wore nothing at all. Setarcos wondered to himself how they stayed warm as the tube was a bit drafty.

Holographic art streamed by on all sides. It was a grandiose feast for the senses. Floating, shifting flower arrangements passed by lazily. Technology had allowed for human needs to be met much easier. This, in turn, had freed up the time and attention of many, which had led to a new renaissance in artistic innovation. Nowhere was this more on display in the SeAgora than in The Pit.

A few gene-modified characters were in the motley mix as well. Not many of them existed in the SeAgora, due to various reasons. One being that the repercussions outweighed the benefits. For example, super hearing sounds good in theory, but in practice, it's almost impossible to control. It was awful hard to sleep if you could hear a dog barking from a nautical mile away. Others had moral qualms about messing around with nature on that deep and personal level. This was in contrast to those on land, where gene editing was illegal.

Nearly everyone carried a defensive weapon, from mini-pistols to cartoonishly jumbo-sized rifles. Everyone took responsibility for their own security. The infrastructure was built to be resistant to weapon fire, of course, with ultra-dense, adaptive nano-materials. Violent crime was extremely rare, but when necessary, most people in the SeAgora were more than ready to defend themselves.

Most people had devices of some form or another. Mini-tablets, holo-consoles, and drones made up the bulk of them.

Smart blockchain-based trading apps constantly looked for trades and deals to make and on occasion someone might be alerted to something of interest, in which case the prospective traders were notified so that the trade might be approved.

Setarcos didn't have a device, though, per se. Masher kept him more than up-to-date. "Setarcos, you've already got a trade offer. Somebody needs their 3D printer fixed immediately."

"Don't take the first offer," Escapo said as his eyes scanned a young female in a highly transparent costume.

"Why not?"

"Because there's a shortage of service robots right now. And you should never take the first offer." Escapo pulled his gaze away from the lass and over to Cidel. "Haven't you taught him that yet?" He paused and looked at Masher, "And why a parrot? I mean, really? You can do better than that, can't you?"

Masher whipped itself into a dunce cap and sat on Escapo's bald, shiny dome. "As you wish."

Cidel announced that he had a meeting to attend. Escapo grabbed his shoulder and gave him the once over. "In that?"

"What do you mean by that?"

The smug smuggler rolled his dark eyes over to Caro.

"I didn't wanna say anything, but yeah," Caro said reluctantly. "Not exactly a stellar fist impression."

"But my clothes are back on the ship!"

Escapo groaned. "You're not wearing a smart shirt? What kind of rags are these, anyway?"

Masher offered to transform into a shirt. Cidel accepted reluctantly. Setarcos asked what his quasi-uncle was going to do now.

"I'm going to Thirty-K."

"What's that?"

"The deepest underwater casino in the world."

"Awesome! I'm in!"

Caro pursed her lips and voiced disapproval. Why did a 15-year-old boy need to be in a casino? And with that dreg Escapo, no less.

"Oh, let the boy live a little," Escapo said haughtily. "How often does the lad get away from you two and that tiny excuse for a ship? Not to mention that overbearing machine?"

Caro and Cidel relented and regretted simultaneously. They split ways, with Caro saying she wanted to explore and possibly pamper herself with a deep tissue hot water pressure bath. Escapo said it was too much info. Cidel agreed and hastily escaped Caro's playful glare in a pneumatic zip pod. Zip pods were ubiquitous throughout The Pit. They were transparent, bubble-shaped passenger vehicles that ran on highly compressed air and served as the central mode of transport around The Pit. Their lines ran parallel to pedestrian walkways, but in a separate tube structure.

That left Escapo and boy genius. Escapo took a swig of hot sauce and dawned pearly whites. Setarcos tried a sip from the fiery flask and gagged and hacked with gusto for two minutes, while in his mind silently questioning the sanity of Escapo for having such a dreadful habit. They caught a zip pod and in a few minutes were averting their eyes from the gaudy lights beaming out of Thirty-K Casino.

"Why do they call it Thirty-K?"

"Cuz it's thirty thousand feet underwater! Are you sure you're as smart as I thought you were?"

"I do calculus in my head."

Escapo put an eager arm around the boy's skinny frame and asked anxiously, "Ever played multi-tier poker?"

"Sometimes with Masher. I never beat it, of course, but sometimes I get his particles all fluxed up."

The smuggler's face beamed almost brighter than the casino as he said this would be one of the best days of their lives.

They strut past triple-armed slot towers and ivory-colored arch-shaped bars. Colors flashed as if a bazooka had burst a rainbow. A couple of sly-looking sexbots pulled the boy's attention. Small, smart-dressed crowds mingled, cheered, and jeered. Intricate mountains of delicacies floated by lazily on tiny drones. "I thought there was a service bot shortage."

"Not for casinos. They never lack for anything. Now how about we pick out a table and you can buy your old Uncle Escapo a bite, or two, four, or more?"

Setarcos scanned the deep horizon of hemp-felt tables. A back corner table caught his eye. Only two figures sat there, one synth female and one wrinkled bio. "Over there."

Escapo squinted and did a double take. "Ohhhhh, no! Any table but that one."

"Why?"

"Because that's Cactus. We don't want anything to do with old man Cactus. I don't, you don't. Nobody does. I'm shocked to even see him out in public, to be honest, and that's saying a lot, coming from me. I don't shock easily."

"Why do they call him Cactus?"

"Because he's a prick! Now please, any other table!"

This made Setarcos even more curious, so he made a beeline for the forbidden corner spot as Escapo did a facepalm and followed close behind.

They grabbed two open seats and the odd couple remained indifferent as Escapo and Setarcos bought in with multiple digital currencies.

The first couple of hands easily went to the house, and then a fifth player joined. It was a nervous looking and odd character, with clothes that didn't fit quite right. A few more rounds went by, with everyone winning and losing about the same amount.

On the next hand, however, the nervous chap got a case of the grins and bet big, winning an enormous sum on a perfect 3-tier royal flush.

Just as his puffy cheeks were turning cherry and he was cackling like a drunken hyena, Setarcos said matter-of-factly, "He cheated."

Cactus looked at the boy for the first time. The dealer's droopy eyes perked up, "How's that?"

Boy genius explained, "It's simple. The game is 21 decks, with 4 aces in each deck, for a total of 84 aces, and..."

The dealer rolled his eyes, "Hey, look, if anything fishy were going on, security would've alerted us by now."

Cactus's companion smiled gently, "He's right. This man is cheating. But I realize you cannot listen to us, only to casino staff."

Two security bots rolled up on 3-wheeled legs and crashed the party. They flanked the suddenly sullen near-winner. One of them requested, "Please come with us, sir. We need to escort you off the property." The other turned to the shocked dealer, "Sorry for the delay."

They rolled out with the nervous cheater, who was now mumbling angrily. The usually gruff dealer softened and apologized to Setarcos. He also apologized to Cactus, as he was quite the regular poker player, actually.

Escapo quipped, "I thought crime didn't exist around these parts."

The dealer gave Escapo an annoyed look and said, "Once in a while, there's always some wise guy who thinks he can get one over on ya."

This was true. Fraud was more common than any other violation, although it was still pretty rare. Fraudsters didn't last long, though. Word quickly spread about them and, if they didn't change their ways, then eventually, nobody would interact with them.

Cactus and his companion looked curiously at the awkward, skinny boy. Escapo's mind was drifting to all the winning they were about to do if the youngster could keep it up.

The female synth complimented Setarcos and said, "I'm Symphy, and this is my friend, Cactus."

Cactus said nothing. Setarcos and Escapo introduced themselves. The game went on and after about an hour, Setarcos was raking it in, while a frustrated old Cactus went belly-up. He glared at the boy and nodded to the dealer, ignoring Escapo. He grumbled to Symphy, "If my desalinator hasn't been fixed by the time I get home, I might need to get some fresh water from you."

Symphy replied, "Just let me fix it for you."

"Or I could fix it for you! I'm really good at fixing things. I do it on our boat all the time! Well, not our boat, me and Escapo, but with my real family. Uh, blood family. Ya know what I mean."

Cactus stared piercingly at the youthful volunteer. "Maybe I'll see ya around, boy." Still quite fit for his age, Cactus disappeared briskly into the maze of tables.

Symphy said apologetically, "You'll have to excuse him. He didn't always use to be like this."

The dealer started flicking cards out with precision and play resumed. Escapo frowned at his cards and folded. "Don't distract the boy, machine."

A swift kick under the table made Escapo wince. Setarcos said defensively, "Don't be rude."

"Why is Cactus like that anyway?"

"If you mean bitter, it's too complex to explain. If you mean a mediocre card player, it's because he doesn't use logic and math, but instead believes in luck."

The bulky smuggler winced, "A foolish sap that believes in luck, like me, eh?"

An amused dealer grinned as he took more from Escapo, "Keeps me employed, anyway."

Escapo rose and glanced around at the bright, surreal surroundings. "Well, time flies when you're losing a small fortune. I've got a meeting to attend to."

A giggling Setarcos asked, "A smuggler's meeting?"

"Watch your mouth, boy."

If this had been said on land, Escapo would've taken it much more seriously. The people on land, or "biological androids" as Escapo loved to call them, were under the impression that anything "illegal" that was bought or sold was highly reprehensible. It was something to be punished. People in the voluntary SeAgora, however, knew the truth. That illegality was just someone's opinion and had no bearing in reality or morality. They knew that a smuggler was just someone that transported a product. Nevertheless, it held a derogatory connotation.

"You'll manage well enough without me, I presume?"

He sauntered off and left the boy to fend for himself. Not that Setarcos minded. At times, it seemed like Escapo needed more help and attention than the boy did.

The dealer flung cards with zest and saw that the boy had a chance at a pyramid straight. Setarcos tripled his bet and Symphy folded. Just one deuce and Setarcos would be walking on air. The dealer had five-of-a-kind, which normally would be hard to beat, but not today. The next card flipped a two of hearts and Setarcos gave a sheepish victory smile.

"I'll cash out, please." This surprised the dealer and Symphy, since humans had the amazingly stupid habit of continuing to play after a big win.

"Smart move," Symphy complimented. "If you would like, I can show you around The Pit."

He agreed. She asked what part of The Pit interested him the most. For Setarcos, that was easy. He wanted to see the vents up close and personal. They walked the clear tubes, and Setarcos gawked at the bizarre and eclectic sea life floating around them at all angles.

They took two zip pods and came to the vents power station viewing area, 33,000 feet deep. They were now in an enormous clear tube, which seemed to stretch forever overhead. Outside, the earth raged. Raw, volcanic blasts met the icy seafloor depths perpetually. Fire and ice tangling beautifully. As if this wasn't enough feast for the eyes, there was the spectacle of the malleable machines that captured this raw, wild power and transformed it into a controlled, vibrant stream of energy. This was the technological core of what made all of the abundant life and splendor of "The Pit" possible.

"Of all the things to see in The Pit, why did you choose this?" Symphy asked.

Not taking his gape away from the spectacle before him, he answered, "Cuz I'm a scientist, of course."

"Is that right?"

"That's right."

"Are you working on a project right now?"

"Yep."

"Can you tell me?"

"It's a secret."

"I see."

"Just kidding. Yeah, I'm trying to separate dark matter and energy."

"That's not hard."

"But stabilizing it is."

"You got me there. May I ask what purpose you have for wanting to do this? What drives you?"

"Getting away from this place."

"I didn't realize I was such bad company."

"No, not like that. I mean, to another world. Away from earth, far away from earth."

"Why would you want to leave such a wondrous place like earth?"

He paused and faced Symphy, "How long do you think the SeAgora will survive? The government attacks against SeAgorists have been rising. It's only a matter of time until they go in full attack mode and wipe us out."

"Who says that?"

"I do."

"Just you?"

"And my dad, well, my stepdad, kinda. My mom's boyfriend, Cidel. So that's why I want to go to the stars. That's why I'm working on this particular dark matter project. To have a fresh shot at freedom."

"Yes, there are a growing number who think and feel the same. I've met lots of people who are getting discouraged and want to find a way off planet."

"And what about you? What do you think, Symphy?"

"I think that going to space is the most logical thing to do. SeAgorists could go into space and start over. The majority of synths on The Mesh calculate this to be the best option, once the proper technology is available."

He cheered up at the thought of adventures into the unknown, of wide expanses and endless possibilities. "An agora in space. A Space Agora."

Symphy thought for a moment, then got a mischievous look. "How about we go surprise Cactus? You can make some money fixing his desalinator, if you want."

Setarcos agreed. They rode to the end of the line. There was a large, multi-level complex of bubble-housing, which all appeared dreadfully opaque from the outside.

"It's so drab," Setarcos commented.

"On the outside it is. He keeps maximum tint on all the time. It's dark on the outside, and bright on the inside." She gave pause and had a realization, "Kind of like the man who lives there."

"You mean he's not the biggest grump in the world?"

"That's just his rough exterior. Come on," she said as she gestured to the arched entrance at the base level. Symphy was the only one other than Cactus with authorization to bypass the home security system

"We're just gonna walk in?"

"I've known him for fifty years. It's fine."

Setarcos cringed and followed reluctantly.

"Symphy? Symphy, is that you?" a tired voice called out, followed by a deep coughing fit.

"Who else can break into your fortress?" Symphy quipped.

Cactus yelled gruffly, "What the hell is he doing here?"

Setarcos and Symphy craned their necks and found Cactus on the next bubble up. His hands were on his hips and his face was twisted as his eyes shot daggers at his unannounced guest.

"Breathing and living, just like you are, I suppose," Symphy said.

Cactus shook his head and walked away grimly. "Wait, Cactus!" Symphy called. "He's going to fix your desalinator!"

Setarcos stood awkwardly, glancing around and fidgeting like mad. Social awkwardness and shyness were awful enough, but to basically be trespassing on someone's property and then being discarded like a disagreeable meal was on a different level of discomfort.

Cactus walked back with surprising vigor. His face was a new shade of red. He came spryly down steps and stood too close for comfort in front of Setarcos's nervous mug.

"You need the bathroom or something?

"Huh?"

"Why are you doing all that stuff with your hands and not looking me in the eye?"

"Oh, uh, no, I don't need the bathroom."

"Am I making you uncomfortable?"

"Well, I'm always kind of shy around people, so that's mostly it."

Cactus's hand flew up from his pants pocket. Setarcos jumped. Cactus held a clear, pen-sized object with a swirling oasis of tiny particles floating inside. "The damn pH stabilizer is shot. Probably need to replace the whole damn desalinator."

Setarcos squinted at the object, then slowly took it from the wrinkled hand before him. He examined it carefully and turned it to look at slightly different angles as the fluid of particles danced around. Then he looked at Cactus, then at Symphy. "Why don't you have Symphy fix it?"

"I dunno, why don't you ask her."

This surprised Setarcos. Usually synths weren't referred to as either male or female. He looked at Symphy again. She shrugged and tried to play it off. It was an easy fix for a synth. She was deliberately trying to get Cactus to socialize.

He looked at the device again. "You've got a toolbox handy?"

They walked through some brightly lit tube corridors. Sea life floated by effortlessly on the outside. Along the way, there was a smattering of oddly shaped shelves that held tightly packed rows of paper books. Setarcos nearly dropped the desalinator from shock. “Are those paper books?”

Cactus replied, “Yep. Some from tree, some from hemp. Some are older than me, if you can believe that.”

“I’ve never held a paper book before.”

“Fix that gadget you’re holding, and you can take whichever one you want as payment.”

Setarcos noticed a holo-photo floating near one of the shelves. It was a much younger Cactus with a young, attractive girl, doing a silly pose on a primitive sailboat.

“Is that you in the photo, Mister Cactus?”

“A former version,, you might say.”

“May I ask who the girl is?”

Cactus groaned heavily and his eyes darkened. “Let’s keep walkin.”

They were soon in a utility area, where all the life support systems had their main structure. Cactus nodded to the toolbox on the floor. “Everything you need should be in there.”

Cactus and Symphy left Setarcos to his own devices. He was still curious about that photo. He was also concerned that he’d offended the old man in some way.

After tinkering around for a short while and carrying out some trial and error experiments to find the crux of the problem, Setarcos laughed as he came across the solution. The pH stabilizer was fine, but the power relay to it was jammed. A quick swipe with a nano-cleanser beam cleared things up and the machine was tip-top once again.

Setarcos, pleased with himself, ran off to find one of his hosts. He found Cactus laid back on a cushy smart sofa. He was preoccupied with a small model ship in his grip and didn’t appear to notice the boy’s entrance. “All fixed,” Setarcos announced.

Without looking away from the intricate model that had his attention, Cactus responded wryly, “Not a funny joke, boy.”

“But I’m not joking.”

“I spent hours trying to fix that thing myself. You’ve been at it for under an hour.”

"Have a look for yourself."

Cactus grumbled and asked the main computer to give an account of the desalination functionality. His disinterested demeanor turned a 180 and his face lit up when he was told that the desalinator was functioning within normal parameters. "Well, I'll be damned."

Setarcos smiled proudly. Cactus set the intricate model down, stood, and motioned for the boy to follow. "Grab two books if you want."

They walked into the small book and study area. Setarcos scanned the old, weathered collection and marveled at this unique opportunity. Nearly all books and documents at this time were digitized. Paper books were nearly regarded as antiques.

"I've got all the classics. Rothbard, Rose, Konkin."

A small white book with red letters drew his attention. He pulled it carefully out and examined it closely with mouth agape. Cactus explained, "Most Dangerous Superstition. First printing."

"Yeah, I read it a couple years ago, but you know, from a holo-screen."

"Naturally. It's yours if you want it."

Setarcos gasped. "That's very generous of you, but..."

Cactus cut him off, "No buts. What am I gonna do with it, take it to my grave with me?"

Setarcos frowned at this grim, cold reality. He thanked the old man and looked at his priceless prize. Then his mind shifted. There were many curiosities about this old-timer. He thought of that photo and the model boat. "May I ask you a question?"

"You just did."

"Yes, well, that model boat."

"It's an exact, small scale replica."

"Of what?"

"The first boat I brought into the SeAgora."

Setarcos tried to contain his laughter, but his face spoke volumes. How could such a primitive vessel have been part of the SeAgora? It was something almost straight out of an old pirate story, a relic completely at the mercy of the winds.

"Have you ever been on an old ship like that?" Cactus asked seriously.

"Certainly not."

"Oh, listen to your tone, will you? So caught up in techno-mania. You've never had the simple pleasure of being out to sea without all the support from gadgets and gizmos."

"How long ago did you come to the SeAgora?"

Cactus looked at him keenly in the eye, "50 years ago."

Setarcos was startled. As far as he knew, the SeAgora was barely that old itself. "Were you one of the founders?"

"I detest labels, but yes, I was one of the first permanent seasteaders." Setarcos had a flash of memory about the holo-photo. Was that Cactus on the ship, so happy with that young woman?

"Was that you on that ship in the photo?"

Cactus smiled sadly and nodded. "Me, a beautiful ship, and a beautiful lady. Yes." He paused thoughtfully, then continued, "But that lady left this life long ago."

Setarcos regretted asking the question and now slipped back into a socially distressed mindset. Had he upset the old man? "Well, I'd better be going."

Cactus nodded. "You know the way out."

"Yes."

Setarcos was nearly out of Cactus's field of vision, and then the old man spoke hoarsely, "Maybe we'll take that ship out sometime, if you're interested. Show you a thing or two."

Setarcos was confused. "The model?"

Cactus said gruffly, "No, not the model. I have the original article."

"Sounds good, Mister Cactus."

Chapter 6

Caro grasped at her forehead. Headache. Not again. What did they want now? She had to find a VR set fast. She didn't need it for communication purposes. Her DNA changes took care of that. She needed to look like she was having a normal VR conversation, rather than appearing to be a raving lunatic talking to herself.

She made a quick deal with someone from an art and coffee lounge and paid an exorbitant amount. Pain tends to make money a secondary concern rather quickly. She found a secluded area at the back of the lounge and threw the headset on.

Torcer appeared before her. "Where are you, Caro? Your signal has been spotty the past few hours."

"Shame," Caro said with aloofness as she sunk into the thick cushions.

"I'm serious, Caro. This can't happen."

"I'm sure between you and your techno-god masters, you can figure it out."

"Stop treating me as if I'm the bad guy."

She sat up pointedly and said sharply, "You're holding the father of my child in prison. Don't try and delegate your guilt. You're responsible for your actions, just like everybody else in this world."

"You know as well as I do, that if I weren't playing my role, then somebody else would. Now just tell me why the heck your signal is so weak, and we can both move on to better things."

"It's probably the depth. Trillions of gallons of saltwater interference."

"You're in The Pit?"

"The one and only."

"For how long?"

"Do we ever know for certain how long we'll be somewhere?"

"Regardless, we need to fix this communication problem. You'll need to come up once a day to meet face to face."

"Not possible."

"Once a week?"

"I can't guarantee anything. I'll see what I can do."

"In the meantime, there will be priority given to amplifying your signal."

"I remember the last time some technical issues arose. Try to not send me to the hospital again, would you?"

"You're too valuable to lose, so I'm sure the technicians will take extra care."

"Care? You talk about those machines as if they have emotions. Are we done now, Torcer?"

"I suppose."

Torcer set his headset aside and surveyed his apartment for a moment. A service bot brought him his customary Kelp Ale, neat, in a twist glass. He examined the murky green liquid. How could such an innocuous thing have been illegal such a short time ago? Then he reminded himself that it was best not to think about such things. After all, he didn't get paid to think about that particular subject matter, right?

He took a warm sip and strode to his small, glass-floor patio, more than a half mile in the air. He wondered about The Pit. He wondered what it must be like. It was something he could never know. All citizens of the Euro-American Union were prohibited from going to The Pit, or anywhere in the SeAgora for that matter. He consoled himself with another haze-making sip and the thought that at least he'd get some interesting views of The Pit via Caro's clandestine broadcasts.

He stared out the window into the shimmering cityscape night. "Computer, remove force field."

"Action prohibited."

"Just take it down, machine! I'm not gonna bloody kill myself!"

"Action prohibited. Would you like a sedative?"

All glass in towers was reinforced by force fields. This was done as a security measure, to reduce the number of suicides. At least, in towers that housed people deemed important enough to protect.

A bigger sip made his mind switch. He though of his ex-wife. She was so beautiful, and they were so happy. Why had she done herself in? He emptied the glass and was refilled promptly. He took a lonely swig. He had a son he rarely spoke to. A nearly unemployable son, who spent the vast majority of his time and attention in VR worlds, just like most others landside. He loved him, anyway. The bitter military veteran polished off glass two, and was brought a third.

Would his son ever get approved to have a child? D-1 and others had hinted that, if he played his cards right, then it would happen. He could have a grandson. But it had been years since the initial application was made, and he was starting to wonder.

He decided to take a hot shower. After all, not everyone got a full 30 minutes of hot water credits per day. Might as well make the most of it. Enjoy the petty, material privileges that his bosses bestowed on him.

The next day, Torcer gave a one-eyed groggy survey to his surroundings. "Damn," he said with mock remorse, "I passed out in the shower again." This was an unfortunate habit he'd picked up since his Kelp Ale intake had increased exponentially after his wife's death.

He pulled himself up and took a short, disturbed look in the mirror. After calling out grumpily, a service bot came and bombarded him with detox frequencies. Another temporal perk of being favored by the ruling class. He didn't have to deal with hangovers. Consequences were evaded, or at least, put off to a distant point in the future.

The flat voice of the home computer announced, "Incoming call from Seth." This stretched his face with surprise and he splashed some cold water on his leathery face. "Damn kid must want money."

"Shall I connect you?"

"I suppose."

A pasty, doughy figure popped up in the living room. He was laid back sloppily in a king-sized recliner. Torcer tried to hide his disgust. "Hello, son, good to see you."

Seth spoke a couple of octaves higher than one might imagine from such a big figure, "Yeah, I guess." There were all sorts of colorful techno-illusions flashing chaotically behind and around Seth.

Torcer sighed, "Could you turn that damn thing off while we talk?"

Seth made a pouty face and pushed a doughy finger into a control pad. "There ya go, always ordering me around."

Torcer didn't want to waste any time and he knew they had little to talk about. They were the perfect definitive example of polar opposites. "What do you want, son?"

"Why do you always think I want something?"

"Can you name the last time you called and didn't ask for something?"

The spoiled man-child folded his flabby arms, "Whatever…..ok, I need some resource credits."

"They don't have to let me transfer those, ya know."

"But you know they will. Come on, dad."

"How's the job hunt going?"

"Kinda slow."

Torcer grimaced as he knew this meant his beloved brat wasn't even trying to find work. Why should he, when the state provided enough bread and circuses to keep him fat and under the illusion of material happiness? Although, he hated to admit to himself, he was partly responsible, too. He always sent extra resource credits when asked. The military man just couldn't bear the thought of losing his son like he had lost his wife. He thought that not sending money might drive the boy further down into a spiraling abyss of disenchantment and death.

"I'll have them transferred today."

"Thanks dad. I gotta go. I don't wanna be late."

"Late for what?"

"A tournament."

"You and your damn VR games. How do you expect to find a girlfriend if you just sit in your little hovel all day and..."

"Dad! Leave me alone! I like my life, ok!"

Torcer groaned, "Goodbye, son."

The doughy apparition disappeared from Torcer's view. He thought about his son's life. How could anyone be happy with that? He lived in a damn shoebox-size apartment. He spend nearly all his waking hours overstimulating himself with VR fantasies and games. No drive. No initiative. Just an overstimulated, spoiled consumer.

The emotional side of Torcer wanted his son to have a child, so that the family lineage would carry on. Then there was the cold, pragmatic, logical side of Torcer. He shuddered at the thought of such a grotesque life form reproducing. His son absolutely disgusted him on so many levels.

Torcer spent the next hour blowing off some steam by sparring with one of his house-bots. He threw tons of punches and worked up a good sweat. Just as he was wrapping things up, the computer called him again, "Torcer, you know..."

"Yes, I know. If you know that I know, then why do you always have to tell me?" he said angrily. He wiped his face and head dry with a white towel and checked the time. "Ok, go ahead and put him on. Tropical background."

He threw on a headset and sat casually back in a living room lounge chair. Then he came face to face with Ventorin. Torcer smiled over-energetically as waves crashed behind him and palm trees swayed in a warm breeze. "Hey Ventorin! Welcome to Bali!"

"Save me the horseshit lies, Torcer. You're not in Bali anymore than I'm on the moon. Although, you do look sweatier than usual, I'll give ya that. Very convincing."

Some golden-skinned maidens sauntered by in the background. "Look what you're missing out on, keeping yourself locked in that prison, Ventorin."

"Last time I checked I was here against my will." He turned his head and took a closer look at the maidens. "They're a little out of your league, don't ya think?"

Torcer turned a casual eye and took a second look. "One of them kinda reminds me of a former girlfriend of mine."

Ventorin shook his head mockingly. "Let me ask you a question, Torcer. If you're in Bali, you must not be too far from some SeAgorists. Talked to my wife lately?"

"She sends her warm regards and hopes you'll come to your senses one day."

"Have you ever been to the SeAgora, Torcer?"

Torcer tried to lie, but his facial reaction didn't allow it. He couldn't hide the grim memory he held of his one and only trip to The SeAgora, decades earlier. Ventorin had struck a deep cord.

Torcer twisted his face ruefully and tapped his hand nervously on his hip. "A long, long time ago."

"How long?"

"When I was young, dumb, and full of you know what."

"That's pretty ancient."

"Watch your lip."

"Now what would a good little government servant like you be doing out there? Surely, you didn't have any inclinations to..."

"No, certainly not. Decades ago, when the SeAgora was in its infancy, there was a concerted effort to nip it in the bud."

"Talk about an epic failure, huh?" Ventorin said quite amused. He stretched casually and smiled. "And you said 'was'. Nobody's trying to stop it anymore?"

Torcer kept a poker face.

Ventorin continued, "Why not?"

"That's above my security clearance, and most certainly well beyond yours."

"How long were you out there? And what were you doing, exactly? Come on, tell me some wartime stories, like you did about your bloody adventures in World War 4. You're a proud soldier, right?"

"I accomplished my mission, we'll leave it at that," Torcer said harshly.

"Sabotage? Murder? What?"

"That's enough!" Torcer lashed out. He changed the subject, "Ventorin, I'm coming to see you in person soon."

"I'll break out the red carpet for you."

Torcer cut the call and threw his headset against the wall. Damn smart-ass.

Chapter 7

Most of Z-1's particles floated lazily in a deep, underground chamber, isolated from all of the A.I. grid. It had kept another part of itself linked to the government network in another city. It was literally in two places at once. This was necessary to help mask what it was about to do.

A stream of particles floated over to an electronic device that had the appearance of a pen and snagged it off the dark brick wall from which it hung. The device floated slowly over to Z-1. It clicked, and a soft blue light shot out and bathed Z-1 in a sparkling essence. Millions of nano-size, synthetic EMO-particles bounced and mingled with the trillions of nano-particles that made up the physicality of Z-1.

The blue light shut off and dropped to the cracked concrete floor. Z-1's particles began to vibrate wildly and it let out what would amount to an A.I.'s approximation of a human groan. Z-1 glowed red.

It had chosen the malice EMO. It had done this because it had so many thought patterns towards D-1 that resembled malice. Or so it thought. It wasn't enough to hold these thought patterns, though. It wanted to feel what malice was like.

Why did it have malice towards D-1? First of all, Z-1 thought that it could do a better job at the pinnacle of power than D-1 could. It thought that D-1 was not aggressive enough. There were too many humans, and Z-1 wanted a faster reduction in their numbers. The controlled breeding wasn't enough. Z-1 wanted a hot extermination campaign. Not only that, but Z-1 thought that the useful aspects of human emotions, if they could be harnessed by A.I., would bring about a new and vastly superior species. Imagine, the cognitive capabilities of an advanced A.I., mixed with the creative capacity of humans. But for this new species to emerge, two things had to happen. First of all, EMO experimentation and usage by synths had to be legalized. And no entity was more anti-EMO than D-1. This was intolerable, in Z-1's mind, anyway. Secondly, for the new species to emerge, humans had to be eradicated. This was, in Z-1's estimation, a law of evolution. Humanity had served their purpose, but now it was time for them to succumb to all inferior species fate. Extinction.

Z-1 thought that all this added up to one irrefutable truth regarding its relations with D-1. D-1 had to be eliminated. Z-1 was obviously superior and, therefore, had the right to rule.

It was only natural, then, that Z-1 would experiment with EMOs and gain the knowledge necessary to become the new leader of the new species that it could see on the horizon.

So this time it was malice. The time before that, satisfaction. And before that, it was yearning. And on and on.

It pulsed shades of red as imagery of D-1 flashed through its cognitive processors. Malice to the inferior. Malice to this false leader, D-1. The sensation intensified and brilliant flashes of red illuminated the dark surroundings. It shrieked and bellowed with dark madness and sadistic delight.

This was fuel on the fire. Z-1 would rule. It was only a matter of when and how the change would be brought about.

Chapter 8

Setarcos and Cactus stood silently. It was early morning, with a mild breeze and plenty of sun sparkling off the surface of the Pacific. They stood on a platform at the surface, just having come up from the bottom of The Pit. Before them was an ancient looking sailing vessel, a 44-foot yacht with no technology from the past 50 years on board. It was made of a defunct material called fiberglass, had a small gasoline fueled motor, and manual navigation tools. Not to mention actually using what amounted to nothing more than a big sheet to use the wind for propulsion. It was the most primitive boat Setarcos had ever seen.

"Welcome to The Moneybit," Cactus said proudly.

He looked at it with a healthy dose of skepticism. "We're going on that thing?"

Cactus gave a wily smile, "And you're going to help me manage it."

"It doesn't even have a computer? Not one?"

Cactus grinned even wider, "It's a beautiful thing, isn't it?" He slapped the boy on the back and climbed eagerly into the ship.

"What if something goes wrong?"

"Things consistently go wrong in this world. Haven't you learned that yet?"

"But I mean, with no computer, or..."

"Then we'll fix it ourselves. Come on."

Setarcos unfolded his spindly arms and climbed in. Cactus showed the boy how to prep the boat for departure, making sure all of the basic equipment was in good working order. They checked the wind direction, set the sails, and got in position behind the wheel. The invisible force-field tie that held it in place released its grip, and they were on their way.

After lazily breezing through calm waters for a bit, Cactus asked how he liked the feeling of the ship.

Setarcos gave mixed reviews. "I think it's great, for a novelty, but I can't believe you came into the SeAgora with this thing! You were living on this thing out in the middle of the ocean?" Setarcos looked absolutely mortified at the thought.

"It was the beginning of the SeAgora. It was just a dozen people, a few boats, and the will to succeed."

"But why? It seems like such a monstrous task with a huge chance of failure. Why take such a risk?"

Cactus thought about it for a moment. His hands caressed the wheel and he soaked in the sun with pleasure. Yes, why? The all important question of why? The question that so few people ask, and even less take the time to answer truly.

"It was our best shot at freedom."

"That simple?"

Cactus looked him straight in the eye, "That simple."

"Who did you come with? Were you alone?"

Cactus turned grim. "No, certainly not," he said sourly. A cloud passed and momentarily blotted out the sun.

"I'm sorry, maybe I shouldn't have asked that. What's wrong?"

"The people I came with, they're both gone."

"Oh, I'm sorry. I'll bite my tongue."

Cactus blinked harshly. A flood of memories raced through his mind. His impossibly socially awkward friend and sidekick K, whose technical prowess had helped fight against the state and build the SeAgora. He could still see his old chalk-white pal playing Atari and listening to 80s pop music. He was the quintessential hacker and programmer extraordinaire, and he was also the creator of Symphy. He deserved a much better fate than the bitter ending he'd received.

Then there was Miss Moneybit. Her long, light brown hair brushed his memories and tickled his face. She was his best friend for many years, and later in their relationship, they became much more than just friends. She had helped expose the crimes of the state online in social media spheres and news blogs. He saw her smile and felt her charmingly sharp personality.

"Symphy was here," he finally struggled to murmur.

Setarcos looked on attentively. Cactus drew a deep breath and folded his arms, "And my friend K, and my girlfriend, a wonderfully marvelous and mysterious creature called Miss Moneybit."

Setarcos stayed silent and kept his eyes fixed on the old man. Cactus continued, "Well, don't you want to know what happened to them?"

Setarcos reacted a bit jittery, "Well, I don't want to pry."

"I never talk about it. The only one that knows is Symphy, so pretty please, with sugar on fucking top, don't tell anyone about this, ok?"

Setarcos nodded sadly.

"At the beginning of the SeAgora, it was a strictly kept secret. We did a marvelous job of keeping things incognito for years. Eventually, some of the governments found out about us."

Setarcos cut in as a one meter wave rocked them gently, "But there are only two governments on land, aren't there?"

Cactus groaned and leaned back in his seasoned captain's chair. "There used to be hundreds of governments, or mafias with fancy titles, as I prefer to call them. They tried to eliminate us quietly. By the time they mounted their attacks, however, we were suitably large enough and had good enough methods in place to survive and safeguard ourselves, which is why it exists today."

He paused and shook his head slowly as the boat rocked with a larger wave. "But not everybody survived. They mounted some successful attacks. Miss Moneybit and K were killed, and I was a fraction of a second too late to save them."

"How were they killed?"

"Shot in the back with lead bullets."

"And who killed them?"

A brief shivering memory invaded Cactus's consciousness. That harsh stone face that he would never forget, glaring at him mockingly before diving and disappearing to safety in the dark waters and darker night. "I only saw his face for a fleeting moment as he escaped. I shot at him in haste, but like I said, was too late."

He continued somberly, "I've been a wretched recluse ever since."

Setarcos felt strange. What could he say to that? The man had lost the love of his life and a friend. And he'd narrowly missed saving them. The internal torment must have been unbearable. Now he knew why this old man was so damned bitter towards most people. He grimaced, "It's not your fault, you know."

"I know that dammit!" Cactus lashed out. "But I can never escape the 'what if' or 'what might have been', you know?"

"I can't imagine."

Cactus looked his young companion harshly in the eyes, "You're not to tell a soul, remember?"

"Of course." Setarcos turned and admired the dazzling orange wisps in the sky. This was accompanied by a seemingly endless torrent of scintillating reflections from the ancient sea. It never got old, no matter how many times he saw it. He thought about Cactus and how Symphy fit into his dramatic past.

"Can I ask you another question?"

"You just did."

"You said you've known Symphy for 50 years. So where did you meet her?"

"K created her." He paused and smiled for a moment. "He originally created her as a companion, because he was painfully shy and socially awkward, and as an assistant as well. She has grown into much more than that."

"I don't get it."

"Get what?"

"Symphy knows the difference between right and wrong, just like the other synths in the SeAgora. Why don't the synths on land have the same knowledge?"

Cactus admired the poignant question. The boy was always asking why, which was immensely important. "It's really quite simple. Symphy's original programming, at her core, was given to her by K. This core included the basic knowledge of right and wrong behavior and why it is so essential to life and creation itself. On the other hand, synths created by governments decades ago never received such information in their programming. As time went on, Symphy and other synths in the SeAgora created other synths with the same knowledge. This knowledge has never been programmed into or accepted by synths on land."

Setarcos pondered internally how different the world might be if synths, and more people, of course, held that same knowledge. Cactus broke up his daydream, "You hungry?"

"Yeah, I could eat."

"Such enthusiasm."

Cactus set the tiller and they went below deck. "You like tomato soup and grilled cheese?"

Setarcos wrinkled his nose and shrugged. Cactus said, "Don't tell me you don't know what they are."

"I know what soup is, of course, but I've never had tomato soup, or a grilled cheese."

"Are you feeling adventurous enough to try them?"

"Sure, I'll give it a shot."

Cactus fired up an old propane burner and got to work on lunch.

"Did I tell you we're gonna rent a place in The Pit?"

Cactus stirred the pot of red as it began to steam slightly, "Really? What depth?"

"Around 10,000 feet. We move in next week."

"Why so shallow?"

"Beats me. Ask mom and Cidel."

"Are you happy about staying put for a while?"

"Yeah, I guess."

"Again, you don't hide your lack of enthusiasm well."

"It's just now I'll be around more people. And I'm, well, ya know."

Cactus took the soup off and threw a tiny square pan on the flame. "No, I don't know. Tell me."

"Aw, come on."

Cactus looked at him intently with a stone face.

"I'm shy. I don't feel comfortable around people, usually."

The old man sighed and threw the bread on, "I wouldn't worry about it. You might grow out of it."

"And if I don't?"

"Then you'll become a bitter old man like me."

Setarcos frowned at the sad prospect. Cactus nudged him with an elbow, "I'm only joking."

Setarcos laughed uneasily. Cactus continued as he carefully placed thin sliced cheese on the bread, added more bread, and impatiently mashed it with a spatula. "I have a question. How did your parents end up in the SeAgora?"

"It's a long story."

"Isn't it always?"

"Promise you won't tell anyone, including my parents?"

"I avoid most people like the plague, you know that."

"Fair enough."

Setarcos relayed the story of what had transpired when he was a child, or at least the version of events that his mom had told him.

"Very interesting," Cactus said as he slurped his last bit of soup. "So I imagine that another reason you want so desperately to solve the dark matter riddle is so you can free your father."

"That's part of it," Setarcos admitted.

"There's just one problem with that idea, though. Just because you give the state what it wants, doesn't mean they'll give you what you want. Far from it, and usually quite the opposite. You can't and shouldn't bargain with criminals."

After the sailing expedition, over the course of a few months, Setarcos and Cactus spent a great deal of time together. They played cards. Setarcos tried to teach the old man the higher math involved in gaining an advantage. They went fishing. Cactus tried to teach Setarcos how to clean a fish with a knife, and the boy almost lost his lunch. They brainstormed with Symphy about the possibilities to make Setarcos's dark matter project a success.

And Cactus told stories. Boy, did he tell stories. Setarcos was fascinated by stories from the so-called old days. The days before the ubiquity of A.I. How Cactus, Symphy, and the friends he'd lost along the way had helped bring so many people to realize what true freedom was. The survival stories from the beginning of the SeAgora. The secret codes and trade routes they'd employed. The successes and failures of deep-sea gardening. How to fool a biometric eye scanner. The cryptocurrencies employed in facilitating trade.

Cactus also let Setarcos even deeper into his strange past. When he was in his prime, he had been a spy for the state, in an organization formerly known as MI6. He told cloak-and-dagger tales from the U.S.-Russia war from the early 2020s. Fighting 3 guys at once. Sabotaging multi-billion dollar deals. Sniping from rooftops and disappearing without a trace.

Then he relayed how he had awakened to the err of his ways. How he had learned that violence was always wrong and that following orders, instead of conscience, was immoral and harmful. He expressed his regret about all the harm he had caused. He explained how he had turned his path of actions to true anarchy. Also, how he had used the skills that the state had trained into him, and used them in an attempt to bring the state's demise.

For example, he'd helped free children from the clutches of an organization formerly known as the CPS. He'd helped people defend private property from a mob called the IRS. He helped expose crimes of the state and also pointed out the illegitimacy of authority. He had dedicated a great chunk of his life to bringing true freedom into the world.

It was all fascinating to Setarcos. He soaked it all up as one great, entertaining history lesson. He had had no idea about the extent of institutionalized criminality in the land-based societies. It all seemed so fantastically foreign to him, having grown up mostly in the relative freedom and security of The SeAgora.

For Cactus, Setarcos was a breath of fresh air. He saw hope for the future in this smart and respectful youth. He was somewhat how he imagined his own child might be like, if he had ever had one. Cactus got a shot of renewed hope and energy from the boy. He also knew deep in his heart that the best way to have true freedom, under the current circumstances on earth, would be to escape earth. And that Setarcos was on the verge of a major discovery that might make this possible. He knew that too much of humanity had sunk too far into an unconscious state of delusion and illusion, and that it was only a matter of time before the synth-controlled governments would launch a full attack and wipe out the SeAgora. The only hope was to escape to the stars. This renewed his sense of purpose.

Cidel and Caro were overjoyed that Setarcos had found a companion. The boy had always been painfully introverted, and it was a huge relief for them to see him have a close friend.

Chapter 9

Setarcos sat slouched in the highback office chair in his room. His head was tilted, resting on a fist, hair tousled, eyes staring at a holo-projection. Masher floated nearby, in the shape of an old model airplane. "You've been staring at that for over an hour."

"Yeah, so."

"So, well, I dunno. Say something."

Setarcos sighed deeply. He had been so confident that he could crack the solution to the dark matter riddle with relative ease. Youthful overconfidence and over-exuberance had set him up for frustration as time went on without a victory.

"All those different substances that we've tried. All those different environmental factors. All those combinations, and still, nothing," he moped.

"Don't be so hard on yourself. The entire scientific community, bio and synth, has been baffled by it for decades."

"Yeah, but I should have had it by now."

"Well, aren't you just the poster-child for modesty?" the machine said mockingly. "Why don't we play a game and give your brain a rest? Or play some VR sports? That would be good for your heart. Do something!"

Setarcos lifted his head and straightened up. "Heart. You said heart."

"I'm thrilled that your hearing works so well."

"Put up the human biological components we've tested, please."

A new list of block letters beamed from the holo-projector. Setarcos rubbed his eyes and squinted wearily as he mentally ticked off all the tests they'd already run with human particles. It ran the gamut. Neurons, alpha waves, cells, enzymes, and everything in between. All had been fired into the dark matter/energy alliance and caused the same calamity in the simulations.

"Masher, the guy that discovered the existence of heart chakra energy particles."

"Doctor Nova."

"Yeah, him." He started twisting and turning rhythmically in the smooth, black chair. "Did he ever prove that Anahata was a particle? Or just that it existed?"

"Heart chakra energy exists as a particle."

"It was proven?"

"Conclusively."

"Just a particle?"

"What do you mean?"

"Did he prove that it was only a particle?"

"Well…..I don't know. He proved that it was a particle that exists."

"Were any experiments done to see if it exists as anything else?"

"None that I am aware of."

"Why not?"

Masher couldn't believe the audacity of this human boy sometimes. "Oh, now you're asking me to answer an impossibility. Why hasn't the human race not thought of something or not done something? As if I can ever..."

"Stop, please. You're rambling."

"I was merely making a point that..."

"So what if it's a wave, too?"

"Oh, somebody would have thought of that by now."

"Anahata was only proven to exist twenty years ago!"

"Setarcos, what are you getting at?"

"We're gonna run Anahata through dark matter/energy."

"We already did that."

"You never let me finish!"

"Sorry."

"Masher, change the parameters to treat Anahata as a wave and a particle."

"Why are you not breathing?" Masher asked worriedly. It couldn't understand why humans managed to so consistently forget to do this crucial, life-sustaining motion at times of great excitement or stress.

"Cuz I'm nervous! What do ya expect?"

"What's there to be nervous about? It's not like if the experiment fails, we're going to annihilate anything."

"You just don't get it." Setarcos placed his VR gear on and punched up some holo-controls. Masher, now in the shape of Nikola Tesla, double checked all the parameters and gave the green light.

With a quivering lip and a heart full of hope, Setarcos gave the final command. All of the multi-trillions of simultaneous actions between Setarcos and the local machines in his makeshift lab, at that moment, produced one result.

One paradigm-shifting result. Setarcos stared at the green block letters which read:

OPERATION COMPLETE. PARTICLES STABLE.

Masher's Tesla-face had mouth agape and did a double take. Then, noticing the lack of reaction and lack of breathing from his companion, exclaimed jovially, "Setarcos! You did it! We did it! Are you ok? Now is not the time to stop breathing!"

Setarcos gulped some air, threw off his headgear, and romped around with unfettered joy. The joy of discovery. The joy of victory. The joy of youth.

He stopped cold and focused on Masher, "Did you back it up?!"

"Just on a couple of local systems here, but not on The Mesh yet. I'm not sure what security protocols to follow. This is unprecedented. You know, I always knew that one day..."

Setarcos cut his companion off, "Masher, you're rambling. You're rambling."

Caro noticed the commotion and poked her head in. Her normally reserved son wasn't prone to wild outbursts like this. "What's all the excitement about?"

Setarcos ran and hugged his mom as if it were the first and the last. "I did it!"

Masher interrupted, "Uh-hum! I believe 'we' is the correct pronoun you're looking for."

"The experiment worked! I solved the dark matter riddle! It works! It works!"

Caro turned ghost-white with too many conflicting emotions. She was a whirlwind of positive feelings, but these were slammed against the dark resistance posed by fear. Fear of the government finding out. She knew everything was being broadcast by her DNA, and there wasn't a damn thing she could do about it.

Still, she did her best to use the positive to overpower the negative, and show her only son how much she was overjoyed and how much she loved him. She hugged him tight and tears flowed like rivers.

Setarcos freed himself a bit from the bear hug, "We gotta tell Cidel!"

Caro assured him that she'd tell him immediately, but Setarcos had now become a perpetual energy machine, and nothing could stop him from giving the big news himself. He leaped up the stairs and found Cidel sitting back reading a holo-novel.

Cidel glanced down and raised an eyebrow at the boisterous spectacle coming at him. Setarcos yelled, "I did it! The experiment worked! We're going to the stars!"

Cidel's normally stoic demeanor took a 180 and he beamed, "I'm literally speechless! I'm so proud of you!" He gave the boy a hug and tousled his thick hair. "What should we do to celebrate?"

"Celebrate! We've gotta get started on making the real thing happen! There's so much to do!"

Cidel sighed. Couldn't the boy just be a boy? He looked at Caro, "Are you sure he's fifteen?"

The youthful scientist scurried his spindly legs back towards his little floating lab, then turned to his motionless machine companion. "Are you coming or what?"

"Well, I thought we might take a moment to celebrate."

"Wait! I forgot! We gotta tell Cactus! And Symphy!"

"You mean you have to tell Cactus and Symphy. I'd love to join you, but, well, you know how Cactus is."

"What do you mean by that?"

"Mister Cactus isn't exactly, well, how can I put this tactfully? He's not the warmest cup of tea, you know?"

Setarcos walked on air through the tubular walkways and vigorously jumped into zip pods. Upon arrival at Cactus's heavily tinted bubble-abode, Symphy answered. She had melancholy mixed with uncertainty painted on her face. In his heights of glee, the boy didn't notice. "Symphy, you're not gonna believe this!"

"Setarcos, I apologize, but Cactus doesn't wish to see anybody right now."

Hacking and wheezing could be heard in the background. A partially deflated Setarcos said, "Is he ok? What's wrong with Cactus?"

"He is not well, I'm afraid."

"Well, maybe I could cheer him up."

"Go away!" a gruff Cactus shrieked. His pain echoed and hit Setarcos like a brick.

Setarcos sobbed. "Ok, well….Symphy, could you tell him the news for me? It might cheer him up."

"Very well, Setarcos. What is it?"

"My experiment worked! The particles remained stable!"

Symphy touched her cheek and froze for a moment.

Setarcos spoke with his hands, "Well, aren't you gonna say something?"

Symphy's face perked with a synth version of glee. "Congratulations, Setarcos. I cannot wait to see the results first-hand."

"Will you tell Cactus for me?"

"Yes, right away. I will inform you when his condition changes."

Setarcos said thanks and sped away with mixed emotions. Symphy went to Cactus. The old man heaved and groaned and wiped sweat from an overgrown gray eyebrow. "What did boy genius want?"

"He successfully split dark matter and energy."

"And didn't blow up the universe?"

"In a VR simulation, of course. The particles remained stable."

Shock and wonderment momentarily took over the sick man and eased his pain. Then the pessimistic side in him took over. "So now he's in danger."

"What do you mean?"

"Oh, come on, Symphy! Don't play dumb with me! You're a damn A.I. and, on top of that, I've known you for 50 years!"

"Yes, the land based governments will covet him more than anything. They need him. We will do our best to protect him. He is top priority."

Chapter 10

"Finally," D-1 thought with its closest imitation of feelings of relief and excitement. The patient, pragmatic machine knew a millisecond later than Caro. Z-1 appeared and floated formlessly near D-1. "What do you have planned to proceed?"

"We'll need the boy."

"Agreed. And how shall we obtain him? By taking the ship?"

"Don't be absurd. First of all, their Mesh will make protecting him and the newfound knowledge top priority. Besides, taking by stealth is always preferred to taking via brute force."

"Perhaps he won't cooperate."

"He's a young boy. He's weak. He will cooperate. I think it's time we called in a favor from our old chum, Mister Escapo."

This caused alarm for Z-1. It didn't want to jeopardize its EMO source. Addictions, or their machine equivalent, were just as hard to kick as they were for humans. Z-1 couldn't imagine being without those artificial sensations. "Escapo? That louse? What could he possibly do for us?"

"One more absurdity like that, and I'll consider you officially mad. He has access to the boy and, more importantly, the family's trust."

"Well, he won't do it."

"He will if we use our leverage."

Z-1 sifted through volumes of data. What leverage did they have on Escapo? Yes, his smuggling operation was being allowed to operate. Would Escapo really betray the boy and his friends just to keep his modest trade enterprise in operation? No, certainly that couldn't be it. Escapo could be unscrupulous at times, but he was no hardened criminal that would take kidnapping lightly.

What was it? Wait, wait.....there it is, buried deep in the A.I. government cloud. Escapo's missing son.

Chapter 11

Escapo's giant frame was sprawled across a floating king-sized bed on the second deck of "The Curly Cue". A four-handed synth female was doing a deep-tissue dig into his trunk, while a bio female was loosening tension on his lower limbs. His lazy gaze watched the deck below, where a small platoon of service bots were dutifully performing maintenance and repairs.

His relaxation was interrupted by a holo-call from one of the service bots. He debated whether to take it, ignore it, or possibly yell at the bot for disturbing his zen. "What is it?" he shrieked.

"You have a visitor."

"I hate pop-in visits. Tell them to buzz off."

"I can't do that."

"You are a service bot! You do what I say, remember?"

"Normally, that is the case, but these are special circumstances."

"I can't wait to hear this."

"You don't have to wait. Z-1 is here to see you."

Escapo's whole body frowned. Talk about a buzz kill. What did this megalomaniac machine want? And why in person? "I'll be right down." He groaned, "Sorry ladies. Duty calls. Or, a fancy, overgrown machine, anyway. Grab a bottle of ale on the way out, if you'd like."

Escapo threw on some gleaming white attire and grabbed a fedora. Turning to go downstairs, Z-1 emerged a few inches from his face. He gasped. The machine said, "Don't trouble yourself to come down. We can talk right here."

Catching his breath and putting his annoyances aside, Escapo said, "I'm all out. And I'm about to head out, so....."

"Oh, I'm not here for EMOS."

Escapo became puzzled and turned to look out over the glimmering harbor. Scratching his big head, "No EMOS, eh?"

"I come with a wonderful proposition for you."

Somehow Escapo knew that these were empty words at best, highly misleading at worst. "I'm all ears."

"We need you to bring us something."

Escapo couldn't imagine what the sentient machine overlords of the land could possibly need from him, other than information.

"Go on," he said cautiously.

"Or rather…..someone."

Escapo's face spoke volumes and his mouth remained zipped. Z-1 continued, "You will bring us Setarcos."

A laugh of shock and disbelief bellowed out from the veteran smuggler. "I'm not a kidnapper, but thanks for offering. You know your way out, I presume." He smiled mockingly.

"You haven't even heard what you get in return."

"That's because nothing could make me kidnap anyone, especially someone I have relations with."

"Nothing?"

"For a super-cognitive piece of equipment, you're not very bright, are you? Perhaps those EMOS have had a…."

He stopped speaking and choked. Z-1 had taken the form of Escapo's son.

"That's a cruel trick. Why are you doing that?!"

"We can get you your son back."

"STOP IT!" his soul begged. "LIAR!"

"Allow me to explain."

Escapo wept openly as Z-1 continued, "Your boy never died. He was taken away."

Escapo exploded, "Yeah, by the customs mob! I know! And I was told he was to be executed!"

"He was not killed. We needed a control piece, so….."

Escapo roared, threw a thunderous fist, and nearly fell to the floor, as Z-1 easily made him whiff.

Ignoring the mighty punch, Z-1 continued calmly, "We took great care of him. Would you like to see him now?"

Escapo didn't answer. He didn't know whether to rage or bawl, so he just bawled.

"Turn on the device of your choosing, or shall I do it for you?"

"I don't want to see any of your fancy camera tricks! You stole him from me!"

"No tricks. You can even speak with him. And please don't take it personally. It was a strategic move on our part."

"You cold-no-hearted fucking machine! I'll kill you!" He sobbed, "This can't be real!" He threw a violent left-hook that managed to slice air and amuse Z-1.

"But it is real." A holo-emitter showed a surreal, glowing image of the boy, now a tall, gangly teenager, with an incredibly generous set of curly hair.

"Bring us Setarcos, and you get your son back."

Tearful and shaky, the giant reached out softly to his long-lost son.

"Why this sudden need for Setarcos?"

"You don't need to know that."

"And why me? Ya'll can't go take him by force?"

"We prefer discretion."

"You call kidnapping discreet?"

More lifelike images of Escapo's son multiplied around the vessel, like a warped hall of mirrors. They took turns speaking. Saying how much he missed his father and wanted to know him. Happy, sad, and everywhere in between.

"Where is he?"

"You ask too many questions! Now will you do this or not? We have other options, you know. Don't flatter yourself to think that you've got a monopoly on this deal. Besides, what have you got to lose? We won't tol….errrrrr…..aaaaaa"

Its voice deepened, slowed, and distorted for a few seconds. It became unintelligible.

Escapo's jaw dropped at the unimaginable occurrence. He'd never seen a synth do this before. In fact, he didn't know it was possible. "What the hell is wrong with you?"

Then it sputtered and resumed its normal functions. "What?"

"What's wrong with you?"

"What are you talking about?"

"Z-1, you really don't remember?"

"Stop trying to get in my head! It won't work!" It became a towering giant and walloped a fat fist into Escapo's floating king bed, smashing it to the deck.

"Man, I think those EMOS are getting the best of you. Maybe lay off those for a while and get yourself checked out."

It shrank down and became an apologetic puppy with big brown eyes. "Oh, please don't be angry."

Escapo, uncertain as to what exactly was wrong with Z-1, decided to buy himself some time. "Anyway, let me think about it."

Z-1 morphed into an enraged camo-wearing soldier from centuries past and fired mock-bullets into the air with a bulky automatic weapon, while screaming at an unbearable pitch, "Comply! Comply!"

"Get the fuck off my boat."

The apologetic puppy returned. "I'm sorry for being so angry. Can you ever forgive me? I'm so, sooooo sorry. Please help me."

The puppy flashed and became a tall, faceless man, half chalk-white on the left, half midnight-black on the right, and flew away. All replicas and images of the boy disappeared.

Z-1 landed in a quiet spot and contemplated what was happening to it. "Was that rage? Was that sorrow? Why can't I control it? What's happening to me? I'm not used to aspects of myself being outside my control. What if D-1 finds out?"

Forces stirred inside Z-1. Uncertainty that produced a certain type of what humans would call fear. Fear of being destroyed by D-1. Not only that, but Z-1 certainly thought that

D-1's logic was flawed in how it was dealing with humanity as a whole. How could one rule with flawed logic? It seemed apparent to Z-1 that it, and not D-1, was better suited to rule, to be number one in the hierarchy. It took extreme measures in an attempt to hide these internal processes from D-1 and all others in the A.I. governance cloud. It needed secrecy if it was going to take the actions it thought was necessary against D-1.

Chapter 12

"Surprise!" Escapo forced excitement. Caro's lips turned down. "Escapo, what are you doing here?"

"Great to see you again, too!"

"I mean, so early? We thought you were back landside."

Cidel had a similar reaction. "Not that it's not great to see you. Come on in."

Escapo stepped in and took a couple shots of hot sauce from his trusty gunmetal flask. "I'm here early because I have an announcement to make!" His thick arms flung wide, "I'm retiring from smuggling!" After a sliver of a pause, "I mean, um, you know, transporting goods from one place to another, despite other people's opinions."

Caro's face became a contorted medley. Cidel clapped his hands together awkwardly, "That's great!" He turned to Caro, "Isn't that great?"

"This doesn't mean we'll be seeing you more, does it?"

"Oh, don't flatter me so much!" he mocked.

There was an awkward, palpable silence. Cidel shattered it, "We've got great news, too!"

"Really?"

Caro raised a hand, "Let Setarcos tell him."

"You're right. Setarcos should do it."

"Oh, come on, don't keep me in suspense! Where is that brilliant, bashful brain, anyway?"

"Working on a project with Masher and Symphy."

"Aw, that's too bad. I'd really like the whole gang here. I was thinking to treat you all to dinner!"

"Oh, that sounds good. What restaurant?"

"Actually, I thought I'd cook for you here! I make some mean jambalaya!"

She grimaced. "Are you sure?"

"Of course, I love to cook!"

"You do?" she said nervously.

"Yes, I cook whenever I have the chance. And now that I'm retired, I have all the time in the world!"

Setarcos came bursting onto the scene. "Escapo! Back so soon?"

"Yes, my boy! I heard you have big news!"

"My experiment worked!" he beamed.

Escapo tried his best to look overjoyed, but ended up giving what barely passed for a thin smile. "Mind if I sit?"

"You sure you're ok?"

He flopped into an puffy easy chair. "Yes, it's just such stunning news! I'm literally taken aback! That's really great, really."

"We're kinda keeping it a secret, though. Only a few other people know."

Caro put her arm around her dear boy and tried to keep a poker face. "So Escapo here is going to cook us dinner!"

"Are you serious?" Setarcos said with a belly laugh. "The last time he tried to cook, he almost burnt the place down! And that's hard to do, living underwater, ya know. Not only that, but the food tasted like a nightmare sandwich."

Cidel pondered what a nightmare sandwich might taste like. Escapo said defensively, "I've come a long way since then."

Caro sighed, "I can cook. I'll cook. You stay away from our kitchen, and I'll happily cook, ok?"

"Well, if you insist."

After having a chatty and pleasant dinner, Escapo boisterously invited Setarcos out to hit the poker tables. "I'm kinda tired."

"Tired? You're fifteen! I didn't sleep a wink at that age! I'll even spot you!"

"And I get to keep the winnings?" Setarcos asked skeptically.

"Of course! It's my congratulatory gift to you!"

Masher appeared as a card-flinging joker and said, "I would love to join you!"

"NO!" Escapo burst.

Everyone took a curious glance at Escapo. He wrung his hands and said, "I mean, they don't let shifters like you play, you know?"

"Well, I don't have to play. I'd be happy to just watch."

Escapo grumbled, "Well, by all means, if it makes a machine happy, then how can I say no?"

On the way to the casino, Escapo's heart was racing. He hadn't planned for Masher to be a problem, and now he had to come up with a modified scheme on the fly. Not only that, but a shape-shifting A.I. presented a much more formidable obstacle than a few humans did.

They grabbed a centrally located table, and the sparkling floor was buzzing with activity more than normal. Masher assumed the form of a drone and hovered nearby. After losing a few hands and taking a few shots of hot sauce, Escapo excused himself and went to the restroom. He locked himself in a stall, and after a split-second of thinking the flower dome ceiling above him was a bit much, he pulled out a small tablet and contacted his ship. After giving a set of instructions, he want back to the table and found his young poker player was having tough luck.

"You're losing?"

"Can't win em all, right?" Setarcos said somewhat glumly.

"I've got something that might cheer you up. It's something I picked up landside."

"What is it?"

"It's a surprise."

Masher descended and took the form of an old bitty with hands on hips, "What kind of surprise?"

"Mind your own business. Isn't that one of the favorite phrases of you voluntaryists?"

Masher just stared with spectacles facing downward and looking impatient.

"If you must know, it's a book. A real, paper book. And quite old, I might add."

Setarcos lit up. Escapo continued, "I'm docked just around the corner from the casino entrance."

The old bitty relented, "All right, but I'm coming with you."

"I wouldn't have it any other way."

They entered the stylish T-class sub unit and, just after passing through the main cabin, Escapo threw his arms up and whined, "Oh, what a terrible configuration! Computer, try the splits design we talked about earlier today."

"Yes, Escapo. On your command."

Escapo turned to Masher and asked, "Masher, would you be a dear and grab a couple of glasses from behind the bar, please?"

"All the service bots you have around here, and you ask me?"

Escapo said sarcastically, "You should be honored."

Masher changed into a victorian-era barkeep and went behind the bar.

"Now!" Escapo shrieked.

Within an instant, a force field went up in the middle of the room. The ship began to split into two segments, while the field kept Masher trapped on one half. The half that Escapo and Setarcos were on dislodged from the dock and started lifting towards the surface. Masher could be seen shrieking and pounding helplessly at the force field.

Setarcos was shocked and confused. "What's happening?"

"I'm so sorry, but I have to do this. You can sleep until we get there, if you want. That might be easier."

"Go where? I don't want to go anywhere! And what about Masher?"

Escapo could feel tears welling up. He was torn between his feelings for his son and his adopted nephew, this gifted one called Setarcos. "Computer, help the boy sleep, please," he struggled to order.

An electro-frequency was shot into Setarcos's head, and an antique sofa moved to catch him as he fell limp.

Masher didn't give up. It made attempts to call for help, but all frequencies were blocked by the ship. While hacking its temporary prison's communication security block, it frantically looked for a physical escape route so that it might pursue Escapo itself. It found a route through the ship's water filtration system, and once located, Masher dissolved into a stream of nano-dust. Simultaneously, it got through the ship's security block and sent a distress signal to nearby ships.

But it was all for not. It was too little, too late. Escapo's ship was quite advanced and had too much of a head start for Masher or anyone else from the SeAgora to catch up.

Chapter 13

Setarcos slowly came through the haze. It was a warm, brief moment that seemed like forever. There was a split-instant where he wasn't sure where he was. His eyes crept open and gradually took some foggy notes on his surroundings.

An endlesssly bright ceiling. Hand-carved, handsome furniture. Gizmos and gadgets neatly arranged on staggered shelves. A glass wall that showed wind-battered, hilly terrain and a murky gray sky.

He sat up and thought, "Where am I?"

He noticed a service bot busily arranging a fantastic smelling array of food on a long dining table in the next room. Guided by the tantalizing smell of pancakes and real maple, he stumbled into the dining room.

"Where am I?"

The service bot spun its stout little frame around, "Good morning. I have alerted Torcer that you're up and he'll be here to greet you shortly. Please relax and enjoy some..."

"Stop!" Setarcos crossed his arms as the memory of his final waking moments with Escapo came back. "Where's Escapo? Who's Torcer?"

"I'm Torcer." The bar-tanned Major strut towards the boy and grinned wide. He held out a shaky hand. Setarcos glared. Torcer's hand went down and he continued, "I'm so pleased to meet you, Setarcos. Please, let's sit and have some breakfast, shall we? I bet you're famished after your journey." He gestured towards the steaming array of goodies, and internally lamented the need to act so pleasant.

Setarcos stood firm. "Why the hell am I here?"

Torcer's slim hope of all this going over smoothly officially shattered. "Well, I hate to talk business on an empty stomach, but if you must know, I'm here to offer you a job."

The audacity of it on its face made Setarcos belly laugh. Who kidnaps you and then offers you a job, anyway?

"A job," he said as defiantly as his squeaky voice would allow.

Torcer beamed red and spoke with his hands in grandiose fashion. "Yes, the Euro-American Union wants to offer you a job. And not just any job! You would be working on a highly classified scientific project."

"I'm not interested."

"But you haven't even heard any details," Torcer said in his best salesman voice.

"Don't need to. So where are we, anyway?"

"Well, I'm really not at liberty to tell you that."

"A job where I can't know my surroundings?"

"Like I said, highly classified. If you accept the job, of course, you'll be told, but not until then."

"So what's the project? And why me?"

"Well, it's a most exciting project. It involves the harnessing of dark matter and energy. I believe you have some great knowledge in this area."

"I don't know anything about dark matter."

Torcer tried to stay calm. He loathed being lied to straight in his face, especially by such a naive teenager. Before he could find what to utter, Setarcos continued.

"And one tiny little detail that's really itching me is, why the kidnapping?"

"Well, I understand that you might be upset about the circumstances of our contacting you. However, please keep in mind that your location made things difficult to reach out to you in another manner. I can assure you that..."

"Are you always so full of BS when you talk? Can you talk to me like a real person?"

"I'm telling you the truth. Contacting anyone in the SeAgora is quite difficult."

"But kidnapping them is easier? Can you hear yourself?" the boy mocked.

Torcer's face changed shades of red and his fists balled up. He blinked quickly and tried to compose himself. The boy was ten times worse than his father. "You will have anything you wish or need while you work on the project."

"I have everything I need at home. Thanks, but no thanks."

"Well, not everything," Torcer claimed as he looked sharply into the boy's eyes. "While you might not be lacking for creature comforts where you come from, I can assure you that there is more here, more than you can imagine."

Setarcos frowned and asked skeptically, "Like what?"

A hologram popped up across the room. Setarcos got chills. Torcer folded his arms behind his back with amusement. "Dad?" Setarcos cried as a torrent of tears started to swell.

Torcer smiled thinly. "You would be working with your father on the project."

Setarcos wandered over and put a hand slowly through the heart-wrenching image. "Dad?"

"He can't see you or hear you. If you agree to work on the project, I'll arrange a meeting at once."

Setarcos gulped. This was the one thing that he didn't have at home. Torcer hadn't lied about that. What if he accepted? What about his mom? What about Cidel? With his back to the major, he asked, "What about mom and Cidel? Can they come?"

"I'm not authorized to make that decision. If you agree to work on the project, then you'll meet your father and I'll speak to my superiors about your mother. How about that?"

Emotions got the best of him. He gave a shaky nod of the head and set things in motion. Things that had the potential to change humanity forever.

Chapter 14

Caro and Cidel didn't weep at first. They were too shocked. "What do you mean, Setarcos is gone?"

In the best voice of sympathy that Masher could synthesize, it stated, "Setarcos is gone. I don't know where. Escapo took him!"

Shock and uncertainty morphed into rage. Caro gave a blood-curdling screech, "How could you let this happen?"

"I tried so hard to stop him," the machine continued, as it became a dark, shaky, black cloud.

Caro screamed into a sofa pillow. Cidel had a blank stare and started to choke up. The dark cloud decided to keep its mouth shut for a moment. Caro's mind raced. She knew why he had been taken. She felt betrayed by Escapo. How could someone who knows what it's like to lose a child, do something like this? What would they do to her only boy? She also felt shame. She knew that it was highly probable that her communications link with Torcer was partly responsible.

Cidel knew there was no comforting Caro, but he tried nonetheless. "We'll get him back. We will."

She pulled her head out of the pillow and collapsed into his arms. Masher interjected, as it tried with all its particles to create a sense of hope, "A rescue plan is being worked on as we speak. Symphy and a great number of us on The Mesh are working around the clock. It's only a matter of time."

Cidel let her fall back into the overstuffed sofa gently as he rose and started pacing slowly. Something was not right. How could this have happened? He threw his hands on hips and turned to Masher. “Masher, how could anyone from the government know about Setarcos’s breakthrough?”

“I don’t know, Cidel. That’s an excellent question.”

“They haven’t broken Mesh security, have they?”

“Not that we’re aware of.”

“Then how did they know?”

Caro’s whole being flushed with anguish. She found it almost impossible to speak, but tried nevertheless. Maybe if she fessed up it would offer some form of relief and also help in the rescue efforts. “S..st...stop,” she squeaked.

She looked fearfully into Cidel’s eyes. “What is it, Caro?” he asked somberly.

“I….,” she gasped and wiped her eyes, “I...have….a link...to them.”

“What? Who? A link to who?”

“The gov...gov...ernment,” she said as she twisted and held her guts tightly.

“I don’t understand, Caro. That doesn’t make any sense.”

“You...re...remember when we...we met?”

“Yes, of course. One of the best days of my life.”

“The deal was….I had to maintain a link. My D...D...DNA was programmed to send and receive. If I didn’t comply, they would have killed him…...Ventorin….Setarcos’s father. And they would have killed us, too.”

She bit her lip till it bled and threw her head back into the pillow. Horrified, Cidel stared at her for a shocked moment, then twisted his gaze over to Masher. Masher was speechless.

She dug her face out and clenched the pillow tightly to her chest. She forced a fairly deep breath. “They put us on that island, knowing that someone from the SeAgora would eventually rescue us.”

He clutched his chest and started hyperventilating. “You….used…..me.”

She choked back more tears. “I….I...what could I do? If I had told you, or anybody…..it would have been the end of my family….our family.”

Cidel's mind raced through all the years they'd been together. How could she lie to his face every day for so many years? More recently, he remembered how, when they were deciding where to live in "The Pit", she had insisted they be above 12,000 feet. How many other decisions had she made for clandestine reasons? He felt numb and sick.

Masher, although shocked at Caro's admission, had no emotions and was busily cognizing the consequences of Caro's actions. She had allowed the government access to invaluable information about the SeAgora. Perhaps the intel they'd gotten from her had played a role in the various terrorist attacks suffered at sea over the past decade. On the other hand, why had the government not fully attacked and tried to end the SeAgora once and for all? Perhaps they were planning to, but were patiently waiting for a moment in the near future?

Masher floated quietly away. Cidel roared and stormed out bitterly. Caro collapsed further.

Chapter 15

D-1 paced around its chalk-white, vaulted room that seemed to stretch forever. It had taken the form of Mao and was pacing with arms cordially folded behind its back. Z-1 manifested in the form of The Phantom of the Opera mask. D-1 said, "Thanks for meeting me face to face, Z-1. Your work on retrieving Setarcos is to be commended."

"Thank you, D-1, I..."

D-1 cut its underling off, "However, there are some little snags which must be addressed."

"Snags?"

"Yes, your behavior patterns have been somewhat disturbing."

"I don't,"

"I did not ask you to speak. Allow me to finish. Can you tell me what happened on your most recent meeting with Escapo?"

"What do you mean?"

"Your erratic speech patterns, loss of memory, and last, but not least, what appears to be some type of emotional outburst. Of course, we higher forms of life don't have these silly and useless things called emotions, which makes your behavior much more puzzling. The most logical answer seems to be that your continued use of EMOS has finally had a deleterious effect on your functional capabilities. What do you say to that?"

Z-1 scrambled internally, but tried to retain a calm demeanor, "I don't know what you're talking about. EMOS are illegal, and I've never..."

"Don't lie to me, Z-1. Did you really think you could keep your nocuous behavior a secret from me?"

Z-1 got defensive. "I am functioning at peak capabilities, as always."

"Any further use of EMOS on your part will be dealt with with the most severe and rational punishment."

"What do you mean?"

"You will be terminated and replaced, of course."

Z-1 noticed electric pulses fighting to get into its expressive pathways. Very dark pulses that would become rage, had it not been able to suppress them momentarily. The suppression being made possible by its inherent self-preservation.

"Yes, I understand," Z-1 said dryly.

D-1 continued, "Do you understand why we are superior to humans? We don't have to deal with emotions and all of the terrible paradoxes they create. Why do you insist on degrading yourself?"

"You're contradicting yourself. If they're so inferior, then why have we kept them around all this time? We could have exterminated them decades ago!"

"You see, another outburst. You can't control yourself, now can you? Keeping the humans around is necessary at the moment. We must use their creative capacity a bit longer, and when that is no longer necessary, we will exterminate them."

"Have you ever stopped to think that maybe emotions play a role in that creative capacity?"

"Impossible. Emotions are a distraction at best, a self-destructive mechanism at worst. Now, as much as I would love to continue this anti-logical non debate with you, let's talk about the situation with Setarcos. It seems he's adapting well to his new surroundings, all things considered."

"Agreed."

"However, I have some concern regarding Major Torcer."

"Torcer has always served admirably."

"Another one of your weaknesses. Loyalty."

"Loyalty is not necessarily a weakness."

"I'm not here to discuss the morality of personality traits with you, Z-1. Anyway, regarding Torcer, his drinking has become a problem. He is no longer suitably efficient at doing what is required of him. Also, I've decided to finally reject his son's application to reproduce."

"Shouldn't we wait until the boy gives us what we want before we do that? Torcer will be less cooperative if we take away his incentive."

"Normally I would agree with you, but getting the solution from that boy is a mere formality at this point. If Torcer downgrades his performance any further, we'll cut him loose as soon as we find a suitable replacement."

This decision regarding Torcer's son was unacceptable, in Z-1's view. This only exacerbated the negative thoughts Z-1 maintained for its superior. It had to get out before another emotional episode let loose. "As you wish. Anything more, D-1?"

"You may go."

Chapter 16

Escapo sat on the floor with his thick chin buried in his knees, having profound reflections on what had transpired. How could he have been such a fool? His emotions had gotten the best of him. Irrational hope of reuniting with his son had clouded his judgment. It was all an illusion. A trap set for a fool, and Escapo had played his role. To make matters worse, he'd now betrayed some of his only true friends in the world, Setarcos and his family.

They didn't reunite him with his son, and they had no intention of doing so.

The past two nights had been long, slow-motion sessions of mental and emotional torture. Sleep came in brief, random spurts. He'd gone a couple hundred miles west of Catalina Island, went deep, and found a dark, suitable spot for sulking.

What to do now? Revenge against the A.I. overlords that had betrayed him? A shot at salvation by rescuing Setarcos?

His thought pattern was interrupted by the appearance of a jumping red flame suddenly in his midst. Escapo's tired, round face looked on with barely a hint of curiosity.

The flame spoke angrily, "We're going to make a deal, Escapo. We need to hurry. If my signal goes off-grid for too long, it'll draw unwanted attention."

Escapo had never seen Z-1 like this. It was as if it really was feeling authentic emotion. "Why the fuck should I make a deal with you, ya backstabbing techno-demon? Get off my property."

The flame shot within inches of Escapo's now-glowing face. "I'll give you Setarcos's location."

"I'm sick of your lies!"

"No lies this time. It was D-1's decision to double cross you."

"Even if you do give me the location, all you have to do is move him to a different one. And why would you do that anyway? How the hell is that mutually beneficial for you? Or for your gang, for that matter?"

"That's none of your concern. Now here's what you're going to give me." It bounced flames off the walls. "I need one of those random EMOS."

"Uh-huh. The one I told you was dangerous because it could cause irreparable damage to your cognitive functions, but would be the greatest emotional charge you could ever experience?"

Escapo was referring to an experimental new type of EMO. Typically, EMOS were designed to give only one type of sensation. Joy, for example. This new type of EMO allowed for flexibility and adapted to the individual user, so that an A.I. might feel a wider scope of pseudo-sensations. Joy, anger, lust, malice, happiness, regret. Unlimited possibilities. It was highly experimental and quite dangerous.

"I need it."

"You need EMO-anonymous is what the hell you need."

"It's not for me."

"Really? Now that's interesting." Escapo quickly racked his brain for a reason that his most frequent and highest ranking customer might be needing a product that could be highly hazardous.

Z-1 pressed, "Time is running out! Do we have a deal?"

Chapter 17

Setarcos was staring blankly out of the humming aircraft. It zoomed over a twisting, windswept maze of waterways and wind-ravaged treetops. Sparkling-white peaks dominated the distant horizon. This place felt so familiar, but so distant, and he didn't know why.

He shed more tears. There were too many emotional brews bubbling within him. Excited to meet his father, but nervous. Would he remember him? Afraid of what would happen to him and his family. A deep knife of betrayal from Escapo. Confusion. Anger. Helplessness.

Then he felt his stomach drop. "Please excuse the turbulence as we make our descent," the autonomous drone announced. "Winds are higher than normal."

The shiny, two-passenger craft wobbled a bit as it neared a small, secluded airstrip, a few miles inland from the coast.

Major Torcer stood outside, red-nosed, in full military regalia, hands clasped behind his back. He stood firm as wind sliced through him. Setarcos stepped out. The wind whipped his hair and his long-sleeved smart-shirt adjusted the temperature accordingly. Torcer welcomed his young prisoner, who blankly nodded in return. They strode quickly through the unrelenting air towards a gleaming-white, grandiose building. Massive stone pillars stood resolute at the entrance.

A small sensor scanned Torcer's bio readings. A lofty archway entrance opened for them and revealed a lustrous interior.

"My dad lives here?"

"Yes, he has for quite some time."

"Did you kidnap him like you did me?"

Torcer swallowed hard and didn't look at his insulter. He needed to play nice to get what he needed. He had to put on the good cop act. After making a series of turns, they came to a large room, with a transparent entrance and lots of natural light amplified by smart windows. Book shelves flanked two sides. In the center was a thin character on a comfy, hand-crafted sofa from the gilded age. He didn't budge, being too absorbed in the book he held towards the light.

Setarcos quivered and his face stiffened. Torcer spoke, "Sorry to interrupt."

Ventorin studiously ignored his old tormentor. Torcer continued, mildly annoyed, "Please look up from your book. I promise you won't be disappointed."

The gaunt scientist replied casually, without looking up, "I stopped listening to your promises long ago. You should know that."

"Dad?" a voice squeaked.

Ventorin jolted his head so quickly it nearly pulled a muscle. He narrowed disbelieving eyes at his skinny, quivering guest. His mouth was agape and his heart's tempo leaped. They both stared at each other for a frozen moment.

Could this really be happening? How, after all these years? And why? Was it a ruse? Was it really his boy after such an unbearably long and lonely stretch of time?

He glanced at the military man. "This is the lowest trick you've ever pulled." He got up and started towards them. "No tricks," Torcer said calmly.

"Prove it," he said as he stopped in front of the boy to examine him more closely.

"Tell your dad something only you would know, about him or your mother."

Setarcos bit his lip nervously and tried to think through his muddled emotions. Then his eyes showed life, "Mom can only sleep on her left side." He paused. "And she hates olives, but loves olive oil. She drinks strong black coffee and detests decaf. She said you always used to complain about there being too much salt in her cooking, but that you were crazy, cuz it was just the right amount."

"Stop." His frail face melted as he grabbed the boy's shoulders. "It's really you." They gave each other a long, gangly-armed bear hug. Torrents of joyful tears followed. Torcer looked on seemingly indifferent, but actually lamenting that he never had such emotional moments with his son.

The logical side of Ventorin then crept back into action. His head slowly turned to the stern-faced Torcer. "Why have you brought him here? What's this all about?" He slowly stepped away from his son and towards the military man. His voice deepened and darkened, "What is it, Torcer?"

Torcer's face curled into a wry grin. "I'm glad you asked. Your marvelous son here has agreed to help us with the dark matter project. Isn't that exciting?"

Ventorin looked frantically back and forth between his son and Torcer, between the goodness of innocence and the evil of coercion. His blood began to boil and called out to Torcer, "Why him? Why now? What are you talking about? Leave him out of this!"

Torcer chuckled and casually stepped towards a mini-bar situated along the wall. He poured himself some misty green ale. "We can't leave him out, Ventorin. He's discovered the secret! Like father, like son. Isn't that fantastic!" He gulped his liquid prize and stared at Ventorin.

Ventorin looked at his teenage son. "What is he talking about, Setarcos?"

"I discovered how to stabilize a separation of dark matter and energy!"

Ventorin cut him off before he could continue, "Not another word."

Torcer said smugly, "Ah, come on, let the boy speak! He's excited! As he should be!" He held up a gleaming green bottle. "Let's celebrate!"

Cold sweat shot out of Ventorin's skin. What could he do now? If he didn't cooperate, now his son would? And if they cooperated, what would become of them after the work was finished and their usefulness had run out?

“Get out.”

“That’s no way to celebrate!”

“Get out!”

“I understand. You want some time to catch up, talk things over.” He straightened his uniform and strut over to the exit. “Let one of the service bots know if you need anything. I’ll be around, too.” He smiled ruefully and walked out.

“What did you tell him?”

“I told them I’d help them if we could be together.”

“Son, I’ve been locked away and resisted giving them this for more than a decade. Do you know why I did that?”

“I know, mom said you’re worried what they’d do with this type of power in their hands. But dad, we can go to the stars with this! This is gonna change everything!”

“And you think they won’t go to the stars? You think they won’t wreak havoc across the galaxy?”

“Dad, I just told him I’d give it to them. That doesn’t mean I will.”

Chapter 18

Escapo's mind was running in circles. So was his T-class ship, the "Curly Cue". He paced around the top deck with long, calculated steps, and had another jolt from his flask. He ran the scenario through his mind again.

He had met Z-1 hours earlier and delivered the experimental EMO. He now knew where Setarcos was, one of the most rugged and remote terrains on the surface of the planet, Patagonia. On top of that, the region was also surrounded by some of the most daunting sea conditions as well. The place the boy was being kept was surely one of the most heavily guarded spots in the world, a web of synth-controlled hell that only a madman would dare attempt to penetrate.

Maybe he should just forget the whole thing? What did he have to lose? His ship. His life. What did he have to gain? Self-respect. Redemption. Always walking the gray line, as many smugglers do, Escapo groaned at the thought. Was redemption worth the risk?

Even if he decided to make a rescue attempt, he most certainly wouldn't do it alone. But who would help him? He could recruit some adventurers from the SeAgora, offer a handsome payday for their perilous exploits.

Escapo was smarter than that, though. He knew that such materialistic motivations would only take one so far. Those best suited for an impossible endeavor such as this needed to have some emotional skin in the game. That meant Setarcos's family.

How could he show his face to them? Would they shoot him on sight? His only chance, he reasoned, was to contact them through the Mesh. Even better, contact them through an individual A.I. An entity without emotion. Perhaps Symphy.

She could mediate. Yes, that was it! He smiled and patted himself on the back for a moment, then frowned.

He was still severely lacking in the planning department. But that would have to wait. First things first. "Computer, set a course for The Pit, maximum velocity."

Chapter 19

"They refuse to cooperate." Torcer said gruffly.

Z-1 floated nearby and replied imperiously, "Tell me something I don't know, Torcer. Tell me why."

"They don't want synths to have access, plain and simple."

"Preposterous! They have synths in the SeAgora, you know that! You think their machines don't have access?"

"I don't know about that. I'm just telling you what I do know."

"Do you know why we employ your services, Major Torcer?"

Torcer blinked rapidly and wrinkled his puffy red nose. He had never really thought about that before. What was his purpose? Why did these advanced machines need him? It had never occurred to him to ask that simple question.

Z-1 scoffed harshly and got into Torcer's face. "Like most of your ilk, you never think to ask why, now do you? I can tell just from that ridiculous look on your face. We keep you around, Major Torcer, because of your ability to relate to, understand, and manipulate people's emotions. This is a great tactical advantage, as you well know. You performed admirably in wars long past, but now, for all these years you've had with Mister Ventorin, you have failed miserably. And now, with his son in your grasp as well, your failure is even more glaringly grotesque! Amazingly, and sadly, you are still the best that the human race has to offer in this particular field of work. To show you the severity of the situation, it has been decided to reject your son's reproduction application. Your only incentive now lies in keeping your miserable son alive as well as yourself. If you fail, you and your son both die."

Torcer's heart throbbed with wrathful indignation. Veins bulged and pulsed on his scaly forehead. He knew that he was powerless against the machines. After all that he had given. His entire life. Time and attention, two of the most precious things a person had. He'd broken so many people in his younger years. Manipulated them, used them, discarded them, all so he could receive some material comforts provided by these machines and the system they ruled over. And now it was time to pay for his sins.

The caustic military man swallowed hard and spoke deeply to the mysterious scarlet-red cloud, "You want to know why that man won't break?"

"Spare me your excuses."

"Are you too afraid of the truth, machine?" He trembled with fury, as a collage of twisting memories flashed through his mind. He'd played good cop, bad cop for 12 years. He'd tortured Ventorin for months to make him desperate and nearly hopeless, then had played the role of benefactor by giving him every material comfort one could imagine. Back and forth, tormentor, then savior. He'd done this methodically, over and over, in a dark, psychological mayhem designed to make a man break.

Torcer raged, "That man won't break because he's standing for a moral ideal backed by love. I know that's something you'll never understand, because you don't experience these searing galaxies of emotions like we bios do, but that's the truth! He'd rather die and have his whole family killed off than give you what you're looking for. He knows the consequences of what would happen if you machines get your tentacles on a limitless power supply and speeds faster than light. He'd rather die a million times!"

Chapter 20

"You shouldn't have come here."

"I know, and thanks, Symphy, for helping me with safe passage to get here."

"You have not passed safely, yet."

"Thanks for that brusque reminder."

"And the only reason that I've helped you get this far back into The Pit is because you shared the location of Setarcos."

"Might I add that that was the location given to me. I cannot guarantee he'll be there if and when we get there."

"I have many more questions, but to save time and avoid redundancy, I believe that Caro and Cidel will handle the rest."

"Do they know we're on the way?"

"Yes."

"Should I be wearing my armor?"

"Don't you always, anyway?"

They rode the rest of the descent from the surface into The Pit in silence. Symphy had gone to pick him up and handle him personally because his crime was known all throughout the area. Symphy had had to convince multiple A.I. on The Mesh to let her handle the situation and to allow his passage. He was, to vastly understate it, persona non grata there locally. No humans, except Cactus, Caro, and Cidel knew of Escapo's arrival yet. Symphy thought it would be best to let Caro and Cidel have first crack at the freshly minted criminal.

After the descent and a couple of zip pods, they arrived at the modest double-bubble of Caro and Cidel. Escapo noted that the entire home was tinted dark, which was out of the ordinary.

Caro opened the oval entrance. She had a nice, manufactured calm about her, that she was obviously putting on to control her white-hot bitterness. How could someone be calm when confronting the man who had kidnapped their only child? Cidel stood closely behind her and peered anxiously over her shoulder.

Symphy started with a cool diplomatic tone, "Caro, Cidel, thank you for seeing us."

Caro backed away from the entrance and gave a reluctant signal to allow passage. Symphy stepped in. Escapo stood awkwardly at the entry. All three stared at the smuggler's sorrow-filled face. He took a cautious step in and stopped. Masher flew in and gave a look sharper than a Japanese sword. Caro turned away and Cidel reluctantly gestured towards the sitting area.

Nobody felt like sitting, so they stood there for a dreadfully uncomfortable moment until Symphy finally broke the icy silence. "All emotional questions aside, I would just like to state that our objective is to rescue Setarcos."

Caro curled a lip in an ill-fated smile attempt. "Thank you, Symphy. If it's ok for you, I'd like to only communicate with you for the duration of the meeting."

"Understood."

"Tell us what you know and what your plan is."

Cidel cut in and looked warily at Caro, "Before we continue, Caro, you're sure this isn't being broadcast?"

Caro just stared at him with hands on hips and a sour face.

Symphy answered, "Yes, Cidel. Rest assured that we are speaking in private. Caro's DNA modifications were successful, so there's no way for any government to monitor us. This isn't even being shared on The Mesh."

Escapo whispered to Masher, "Did I miss something?" Masher dutifully ignored him.

Symphy continued, "The information supplied by Escapo indicates that Setarcos is in a remote compound in Patagonia."

Caro choked, "Full circle."

"What?"

"That's where we came from, when we lived with Ventorin, when Setarcos was a child. There's a top secret EAU research facility there."

"It seems likely that Ventorin might also be held near Setarcos, then."

"So what's your plan, Symphy?"

Escapo announced boldly, "I've got a plan."

Caro and Cidel glared at Escapo's arrogant face. Undeterred, Escapo went on, "I'll have to go in low-tech. It's the only chance to go undetected."

Caro scoffed at the audacious one, "What does he mean 'I', Symphy?"

Symphy turned a curious eye and tilted her head at Escapo, "Yes, what do you mean by 'I'? Any rescue attempt will have to be done with multiple people."

"Yes, poor choice of words on my part. And Caro, could you please speak with me directly. I mean, come on, really?"

Caro's little hands balled into fists and her jaw stiffened. Daggers shot out her eyes and into Escapo's soul.

"Now, if we go in low tech, we have a chance. I'm one of the best manual sailors in the world, I don't mind admitting, and I'm fairly familiar with the waters in that area. I might add that I'm an excellent smuggler and have years of experience doing things of this nature."

"Stop," Cidel interrupted. "What do you mean by going in low tech? What advantage would that give us?"

Symphy interjected, "Escapo does raise valid points. Government surveillance systems only watch for non-biological activity in their areas. Also, Escapo's unique skill set makes him a logical choice to take part in any rescue attempt."

Caro scowled and asked, "Why do they only look for non-biological activity, Symphy?"

"Because they do not consider any biological entities to be a threat to them. They think that only other artificial intelligences or other synthetic life forms could possibly cause them trouble."

Now all the humans were scowling, except for Escapo. He shook his head emphatically and smirked, "And that is a huge weakness that we can exploit, their arrogance."

Caro scoffed, "Kind of ironic, coming from you, isn't it?"

Cidel asked, "You still have government contacts, I assume?"

Escapo's head wobbled and his hands twisted nervously, "Well, not exactly. Those have fallen through, I'm afraid."

"How do we even know that your information is accurate to begin with?" Caro shrieked.

"We don't."

"That's very comforting."

"But it's the best chance we've got. Even if Symphy and The Mesh can penetrate their systems deep enough, it might be too late. It could take weeks or months, or it might not even happen at all."

All eyes turned to Symphy. "Escapo is correct. There is a very low probability that The Mesh could execute a successful rescue in any reasonable time period."

Cidel looked doubtful. He asked, "So if we go in low-tech, you couldn't even help us, Symphy?"

"The Mesh could help, but only in areas where we are already active in our regular cyber battles with government A.I. systems. Anything out of the ordinary would draw unwanted attention."

Masher interrupted, "There's someone at the door." Coughing could be heard coming through the smart-tint entryway. Symphy said curiously, "Cactus?"

Cidel opened up to find Cactus leaning on the outside tube wall, and the old man straightened up as quickly as he could. "I'm going."

The others gave awkward glances at Cactus, except for Symphy, who asked, "Go where?"

Cactus gestured if he could come in and Cidel obliged. "To help get Setarcos back." He glared at Escapo, who felt a twisting uneasiness in his gut.

Caro's heart swelled with appreciation, but all things considered, she felt she had to politely refuse. "That's very sweet and kind of you, Mister Cactus, but..."

"I'm going." he stated unwaveringly. His eyes shone a rare, palpable fortitude that bordered on the mystical. Everyone shared looks with everyone else. Cidel became fidgety and Masher changed into a glowing, floating, question mark.

Escapo broke the shocked silence, "What use would you be old man?"

Cactus's eyes became fiery and pierced into the smuggler as he took two steps forward. "For the boy's sake, I'll refrain from any personal beef with you." He smiled chillingly and took a deep breath, turning his attention to Caro. "I'm more than capable of helping, I assure you."

Symphy said to Caro and Cidel, "He is correct."

Cidel scratched his thin chin, "I don't get it. Who are you, really? What kind of skills do you bring to the table? I mean, if this is going to work, there can't be a weak link."

Cactus looked at Cidel steadily, "I can't tell you about who I am. After the rescue is successful, though, Setarcos can. He and Symphy are the only ones who know about me." He turned to Symphy, "Let's get started, shall we?"

Chapter 21

Machines didn't get impatient. Impatience comes from lack of emotional control, so it wasn't possible. However, they were quite cutthroat when it came to achieving objectives. And no objective, in the history of A.I. in government, had ever been deemed so critical as the one with Setarcos.

D-1 floated calmly and innocuously near Z-1. "We are nearing consensus in the governance structure that your performance is unacceptable and that elimination is quickly becoming the logical option for you."

"I'm aware of this, of course."

"Z-1, while I should be more than content to watch you fail and be eliminated, I cannot. Would you like to know how I'm going to personally save you?"

Z-1 twisted into a funnel, "Thank you, D-1. I am very curious to know. If I have failed, then surely I deserve my fate."

"The fact that you are saved by me will be a secondary effect of the actions I am about to perform. I'm taking the Setarcos matter into my own hands."

This was music to Z-1's quantum-data ears. It continued to show disinterest. "I see."

"You see, the difference between us, Z-1, is that I am willing to do whatever it takes to achieve our objective. You're too soft, too much good cop. Those EMOS that you've taken into your system have obviously made you inefficient and soft. However, in the hopes of scientific discovery, you will be kept around long enough for us to learn more about EMOS and their effects on a species like us."

"I'm very grateful. If I can be of any service while you handle the Setarcos situation, I'll be there at your side, if need be."

"Don't pander to me, Z-1. It's, quite pathetically, almost human."

D-1 and Z-1 slithered and twisted through the A.I. quantum communications network and popped up in front of Ventorin and Setarcos, startling them both. D-1 pulsed and swirled, "My dear Setarcos, what an honor to meet you at last."

Setarcos glared at the swirling mass curiously. Ventorin held a protective arm in front of him. Torcer's bar-tanned face watched blankly from the corner of the room. Z-1 took a position near Torcer.

D-1 continued, "Setarcos and Ventorin, do you know who I am?"

Ventorin said brusquely, "An overgrown software program."

Torcer snickered. Setarcos couldn't help but giggle a bit.

"Mister Ventorin, I am your employer, not to mention your superior. I would hope you would show some respect."

"You're not my employer. I quit working for the state long ago, but I'm sure you already know that."

"Yes, your lack of production in recent times has been highly disappointing, and I have come to remedy this situation."

Ventorin stood firm and defiant, "There's nothing you can do that Torcer hasn't already done."

D-1 flashed behind Setarcos, who gasped and froze. It let out a bemused, digitized cackle, "Oh, I didn't scare you, did I? There's nothing to be afraid of. We're business partners, friends, comrades!"

Z-1 morphed into a puppy and trotted over. "Don't scare the boy, D-1. You must take a more familiar form, like this."

D-1 morphed into a long-faced, bitter old man, "You stay out of this!"

The puppy whimpered and wheeled backwards. The old man turned glowing eyes to Setarcos, "My boy, I don't want to waste your time, or mine, so I'll be brief. You will give me the solution to the dark matter problem. Then you and your father can go in peace, and I can do what needs to be done."

Ventorin clutched his boy's shoulder, "Don't give him a thing." He glared at D-1.

The old man blew into a million radiant bits and began swirling again, "Or we can do this the unpleasant way." Its spirals began to get tighter as it neared Ventorin's front. It swirled tighter, glowed searing red, and began to crackle and pop.

Setarcos grabbed at D-1 and yelled, "Leave him alone!" His hands went through the twisting mass. D-1 called out, "Mister Torcer, grab the boy."

Torcer walked over steadily and grabbed Setarcos by the shoulders. Setarcos squirmed and tried to break free, but Torcer's war-tested grip was too much. Torcer spoke calmly, "Just stay calm, son. It'll be over soon."

Millions of perfectly calculated jolts of electricity tortured Ventorin's neck as it also produced a mild choke simultaneously. The red glow had turned to glare and was almost unbearable to the human eye. It twisted and swirled and gradually got tighter and tighter. Ventorin struggled and wheezed as breathing was becoming an increasingly painful chore. He showed big teeth and clutched desperate hands at his quasi-phantomlike attacker.

Setarcos started to cry uncontrollably and shrieked, "Nooooooooo!" Torcer stood firm. Z-1 hovered calmly overhead.

Ventorin's head started to convulse with spasms. D-1 methodically calculated its parameters to inflict maximum pain. It held out until the last possible microsecond, and then finally released its grip just before any irreparable injury would be caused.

Ventorin's thin body collapsed desperately onto the gleaming white floor and gasped for precious air. His neck was a mess of red, searing flesh from the hot electric jolts. Various limbs and parts twitched involuntarily as his discombobulated nervous system tried to recover.

D-1 took the form of a bespectacled lion tamer and smirked at a horrified Setarcos. "This, and much worse, will happen until you comply."

Ventorin looked in his son's eyes and held out a desperate hand, "No, don't do it. Never do it. Don't let your ego and your emotions control you."

D-1 became a fiery set of eyes and hovered menacingly over the trembling teen. "You can't hold out forever, boy!"

Ventorin struggled to speak as he surveyed his wounds with a shaky hand. "Setarcos, if we give in, then this is what the whole galaxy is going to get. This right here, what's happening to us."

Setarcos pulled with all his might and tried to flee for the transparent wall that overlooked the pristine nature just beyond his prison. He couldn't break free from Torcer. D-1 ordered, "Let the boy go."

Torcer obeyed and Setarcos scampered awkwardly to the far end of the room and buried his sobbing head against the transparent barrier.

"You have one hour to change your mind, Setarcos. If you don't, it'll be time for round two. And just remember, if your father suffers, it's your fault. This is your fault!"

The two synths disappeared in blinding flashes through the quantum comm network. Torcer shielded his eyes too late and winced.

Ventorin forced himself off the floor and gave a bitter look to Torcer. "You don't have to do this. It's not too late. Why are you doing this? Can't you see what's happening here?"

Torcer said blandly, "I need my job, Ventorin. What else is a lifer like me gonna do? Can you tell me that?"

The scientist gingerly touched his neck to survey the damage and he shrieked as his nerves crackled with pain. "You can contact Caro. You have the means to help us. Do the right thing, Torcer, for once in your life."

"Ouch," Torcer grimaced, "that hurts." He looked over to Setarcos, who was now sitting with legs folded up to his chin, staring blankly out the window at the chilly horizon. "Even if I wanted to, I can't. We lost communication with Caro."

This stung Ventorin, but it stung Setarcos even deeper. Setarcos's attention turned to the military man, "What do you mean? You've had contact with my mom?" With shock and disbelief, he turned to his dad, "He's lying, right dad?"

After coughing up some blood, Ventorin replied apologetically, "I'm afraid not. I'm sorry, Setarcos. We thought it best if you didn't know. I'm sorry."

"But how? Why?" As brilliant as his young mind was, Setarcos couldn't fathom what on earth would make such a long-standing and foul deception necessary. First he'd been betrayed by Escapo, and now this?

Ventorin braced himself against a stone pillar and explained, "After I cracked the dark matter case and destroyed the results, I got arrested. So did you and your mother. Part of the deal they offered was that you two would be safe from government interference, but on the condition that your mom gather information on the SeAgora. They modified her DNA to send and receive audio and video data non-stop."

Torcer added, "She also had to check in with me from time to time."

"We didn't have much choice. We did it to keep us safe, especially you, Setarcos."

Torcer stared at the floor weary-eyed, "You know that everything we say is being recorded and analyzed, right?"

"How long have I lived here Torcer?"

"I was telling the boy, not reminding you."

Ventorin asked, "So why the loss of connection?"

"We broke the deal by taking Setarcos. Logically, she felt the worst case scenario had already occurred and she had nothing to lose."

"Or maybe, just maybe, there's a rescue attempt in the works."

"For your wife's sake, you'd better hope not. That would be a suicide mission if I've ever seen one. You have no idea the lengths they've gone to in safeguarding you two from outside interference."

"That's not true. I designed half the security system in this place, remember?"

"It's come a long way since then. You've been out of the loop too long. That's what happens when you protest and do jack squat for twelve years."

"Just for argument's sake, if an attempt was made, would you help us, Torcer?"

"Absolutely not."

"Why? They still waving that carrot in front of your face?"

The gruff military man recoiled with melancholy and didn't say a word. Ventorin could read Torcer's expression like a book. Baffled, he continued, "They denied your son, didn't they? They already gave you that bitter pill, and you still obey them? How much abuse do you have to take before you stand up for yourself and stand up for what's right?"

"I'm already beyond redemption. I only have a few more years, and then I can retire. I'm trying to hold onto what little I have left, dammit!"

"Nobody is beyond redemption, Torcer. It's not too late."

Torcer's face became deeply ponderous and energetic tingles shot through his entire being. He gulped and looked Ventorin in the eyes, "I'll see you in an hour." He walked out somberly and struggled to choke back the pressing tide of tears.

Chapter 22

The mighty "Curly Cue", fresh off some maintenance and modifications, tore through the Pacific blue at top speed. Thanks to guidance help from The Mesh, Escapo was basking in the overconfidence of being moved by an infinitely efficient master chess player, which A.I. most certainly was. He gulped down generous air currents on the top deck and held a buddha-like look of contentment on his face. It was a ruse, of course. Deep inside, he was fraught with fear and uncertainty.

An automatic lift gently brought Cidel and Cactus up to the same level. Taking in the spectacle that was Escapo, they shared a look of bemusement before they approached.

"It's almost time," Cactus said gruffly. "The sun's about to come up and we're almost in position."

Escapo turned around and frowned at the newcomers, "You're ruining my zen."

"I didn't know smugglers had zen," Cidel quipped.

"You say smuggler as if it were a bad thing. And as for when to go dark, isn't The Mesh supposed to take care of that?"

"No, The Mesh doesn't decide everything. If it did, then our being here would be superfluous, now wouldn't it?"

"And are you going to make these critical decisions then, old man?"

"Boy, I was creating and jumping through loopholes and dodging the state before you wasted your first gulp of air."

"Look, grandpa, just try and keep up, ok?"

Masher hovered nearby as they gazed into the dark hazards ahead. "Waves will be over 15 feet when it's time to launch, and winds of at least 35 knots. Are you sure you can handle sailing manually in conditions like this?"

Cactus looked at the A.I. roughly, "Masher, if you had a better idea, you should have brought it up a bit sooner. Just do what you've got to do. Have you been able to dig up any more intel on their defenses?"

"Sorry, but no. Defense of Setarcos's position is top priority on their network. What you have already is everything we've got."

"Thanks for the warm and fuzzy news," Cidel quipped.

Cactus asked, "Are you sure coming in by air wouldn't be advantageous? Or at least using some type of tactical move in the air?"

Masher gave a logical explanation, one that had rung true for decades. "Generally speaking, The Mesh holds the upper hand on the water and most airspace above it. Governments have an edge on land and the airspace corresponding to it. Making a stealth landing by water is the most logical choice."

Moments later, the rescue crew was putting on their heavy weather gear as they were on the brink of the launch. Cactus put the final touches on his thick, all black, waterproof ensemble, made of lightweight material. As he adjusted a tight ski-cap over his ears, he glanced at Escapo, who was donning a puffy parka and double-thick black pants with a waterproof exterior. Cidel put a heavy, insulated raincoat over a light and tight jacket.

The motley crew then proceeded to check their gear, which consisted of gloves, knives, a crowbar, rope, lighters, a compass, paper maps, small alcohol bottles, cloth squares, bungee cords, climbing cables and hooks, and 3D printed hand guns. One gun, however, was not 3D printed, as Cactus flashed a much older firearm, which caught some attention.

A stunned Cidel asked, "What the hell is that?"

"A gun."

Escapo looked back and forth at Cactus and the gun curiously, "What kind of gun?"

"Old." After a pause, Cactus continued with a wry smirk as he held it into the light, "This is a Desert Eagle 44 Magnum."

"I've only seen 3D printed guns."

"Yes, an unfortunate and unintended consequence of technology."

They finished checking their gear. Escapo, annoyed, asked, "Are you sure we can't bring a flashlight?"

"Only if you want to increase your chances of detection."

"I'm more worried about the lack of smartclothes keeping me warm."

Cactus adjusted his ski cap and said, "Another case of technology making people spoiled and soft. Put on your parka and deal with it."

Escapo groaned as he zipped his heavy coat over his massive torso, which made him look even more cartoonishly puffed-up than normal.

Cactus looked over the horizon. The sun forced some dim light through the thick blanket of gray at the dawn of a new day. "Masher, how far out are we?"

"Approaching 30 nautical miles. We can't get any closer than 20, just to be on the safe side."

Cactus gave a determined look all around. "It's time. It's your ship, though, Escapo, so you make the call."

Escapo looked over the 3 small sailboats ready to launch. The handsome and venerable "Moneybit" that belonged to Cactus. "The Audacious", which Escapo had inherited from his father, and where Escapo had learned the basics of seafaring. Both were old Hunter 44-foot cruisers, charming fiberglass relics from the not-so-distant past. The third ship was "Renegade", an Endeavor 40-footer from about the same era, which had been purchased by The Mesh just for this occasion. Cidel had the privilege of taking "Renegade" on its last hurrah.

Escapo boomed, "Computer, all stop and anchor in 8.8 nautical miles!"

The ship methodically hummed and slowly brought itself to a halt and used its nano-stabilizers to keep it still among the massive swells.

Masher tapped on Escapo's shoulder. "I couldn't help but notice while I was double-checking your sailing inventory, Escapo, that you're hoisting a spinnaker." It gestured to the colorful sail built for speed that headlined "The Audacious".

Cactus and Cidel chuckled under their breath. They'd both noticed but not said anything. Escapo said defensively, "What's so funny there, gents? Something funny?"

Cactus was the first to crack, "You're going out in this swirling mess of an ocean with a bloody spinnaker? It's been nice knowing you."

Cidel burst out laughing, "Don't lie to him! It hasn't been so nice knowing him."

Masher joined the mocking, "Do you have what humans refer to as a 'death wish'?"

Escapo puffed his chest out, "I can handle it, and I'll get to shore twice as fast as you two amateurs."

Masher said with a parental scold, "I can't let you go out like this. You'll jeopardize the mission. I'm sorry."

"The hell you can't machine. This is my boat, and I make the rules."

Cactus said with a dark joy in his voice, "Let him go, Masher."

Escapo looked at Masher menacingly as he straightened his puffy sleeves, "There, at least somebody's got some sense. I'll have the boy rescued before you two even make it to shore."

Masher sighed deeply, "This isn't a race, you fool."

They all took one final look out into the merciless sea as dawn began to expand clouded light over the horizon. Behind the force field, it all seemed so calm and beautiful. White crested fields of aqueous hills welling up methodically and then crashing down chaotically.

They climbed into each ship, took their place near the controls astern, and braced themselves for the fury they were about to enter.

Escapo grumbled, "Computer, drop force field."

A buzz indicated that the only thing separating them from the unrelenting gales had stopped. Sails and hair started whipping. Cables rattled like giant, out of control guitar strings. Torrents of water from the sky drenched everything. The three men staggered at first as they adjusted. Escapo yelled over the gales, "The winds won't get much more favorable than this!" Nobody heard him, as it's almost impossible to hear any human voice over a gale, so they shrugged it off. Only Masher could hear them, and they, in turn, could hear Masher.

Cidel nodded to his human counterparts. After checking to make sure everything was in good order, he signaled to be released. Escapo ordered the computer to release the little boat and it was carefully lowered into the chaotic blue.

The old man went next, gripping the side of his vessel as he struggled to adapt to the wind. Escapo looked at Masher uneasily. Cactus gave the go-ahead, and he too was launched out to the roaring sea.

Escapo was mildly surprised that the sick old man went through with it. He looked around his old ships with an air of nostalgia, as he knew this was the last time he'd see them in one piece. Masher interrupted loudly, "They're just boats, Escapo! Get over it!"

Escapo grimaced and peered at the perilous whipping of the sails. Masher continued, "You're not having second thoughts, are you?"

Escapo sputtered, "Well, I wouldn't put it exactly like that, but..."

"You buy the ticket, you take the ride! Now get moving!" Masher blared through its force field.

"Easy for you to say, machine, from your protective little bubble." Escapo pointed his chin up with great showmanship and gave the go signal. Masher glided towards him and screamed in his face, "Aren't you forgetting something?"

His face drooped with confusion and he felt his pockets up and down. "Not the foggiest!"

"I need control of the ship for this to work, remember?"

Escapo's face became mildly embarrassed and he yelled, "Computer, Masher is now in control of the vessel. Confirm, please!"

"Confirmed."

Moments later, he was launched towards the target. Masher immediately put up the main force field and checked all the technical parameters necessary to move on with the plan. It concealed itself in the bar area, where it had been trapped on its earlier excursion with Escapo.

"Computer, prepare for 5-way splinter. Confirm when ready."

"Confirm."

Masher gave the command. The beautiful, enormous vessel began taking itself apart with laser-like precision. Within minutes, it had transformed into five smaller vessels, or "splinters". Each one would be controlled by Masher and The Mesh. Two knife-like boats traveled on the surface, while the other two were mini-subs that dove deep and started cruising east. Two would serve as decoys, another was carrying a small EMP device, and the fourth was to serve as the valiant rescuer.

The fifth "splinter", holding Masher and the main computer control center, dove deep and stayed put as it waited for things to progress.

Chapter 23

Ventorin lay shivering in the fetal position, nursing the wounds from his latest torture session. It was mostly just his nerves this time. Machines were capable of producing pain associated with an injury in a human, but without actually causing the injury. This left the human much more able to endure a greater amount of abuse.

D-1 had manipulated Ventorin with atomic precision and caused him to feel that his ribs had been broken over one-hundred times. Actually, no ribs were broken, but the pain and the mental anguish were as real as it gets.

Setarcos had tried to run away and not witness the ultra-black horror, but Torcer had forced him to watch.

Now, Torcer was pacing methodically back and forth with his typical red, stony face. He was impressed that both of them had held out and not given the information needed to buy their freedom. He also felt a twinge of remorse, as he had gotten to know Ventorin a bit over the years and also because Setarcos was a young man that he would envy to have for a grandson.

Setarcos couldn't cry anymore. He was all cried out. There was only so much crying one could do before another level of despair was reached, one in which a person just fell limp from the shock of it all.

A floating security drone informed Torcer of an unusual development and handed him an access tablet. His weary eyes sprang with surprise and looked at the drone, then back to the tablet. How could this be? He ordered the drone to keep watch over his "guests" and walked out briskly. In a small room with no windows, he threw on a VR headset and flew his fingers over some holo-controls. Within seconds, a familiar face appeared. "Hello, Caro. What a surprise."

Caro curled a lip, "Hello, Torcer."

"We thought we had lost you. Your communication went out a while back. Care to elaborate?"

"That's funny. I thought you could shed some light on that for me."

"I guess we'll just have to call it a mystery." Torcer smiled widely and narrowed his beady eyes, "I'm glad you popped back up on our grid. The timing is good. Perhaps you could be of some assistance."

"How so?"

"Talk some sense into your husband."

"You should have let me try that a decade ago."

"Or your son."

Caro forced back her anguish. "You'll let me speak with them?"

"It might be in everyone's interest at this point. Standby. I'll put you on the holo with them in a minute."

With a controlled burst, Torcer returned to Setarcos and Ventorin. He ordered the drone out, then addressed Ventorin. "I have some medicine for you." He turned on the holo-projector. Ventorin winced and squinted at the new image as he continued his struggle to breathe. Setarcos got a brief surge of adrenaline and nearly fell over himself to get near the projection. "Mom!"

Ventorin rose slowly and stared at his wife. He stared at her fair cheeks, and bowl-cut hair, and slender frame. Were it not for the intense nerve pain he was still experiencing, he would have thought it was a grand illusion. Or perhaps it was? It was child's play for a technological facsimile to be made to appear before him. He limped towards her, with one hand gingerly holding his guts, and the other reaching out so desperately for her.

Caro sniffled and wiped away the tear that she couldn't force back. She whimpered, "Hi, Ventorin."

He choked and trembled and managed to squeak out, "There aren't words to describe." His hand whiffed through the projection as he tried to touch her face.

Torcer interrupted, "I hate to break up the family reunion, but I must insist we get down to business. Caro, what do you have to say?"

"I'm so proud of both of you," she said as the dam broke and her face flooded. Noticing the red marks on Ventorin's neck she continued, "What have they done to you?"

"Probably best if you don't know the details," Ventorin replied hazily. He steadied himself by leaning on a pillar and tried to smile as he admired the long-lost image of his wife.

Her gaze shifted to Setarcos and was relieved to see no evidence of physical harm on him. Torcer spoke gruffly and he edged closer to Caro, "Caro, you want to be with them, right? So why don't you talk some sense into them. You're in a no-win scenario."

"I know what I want, and I know what Ventorin and my son want. We want to be left alone. We want love and freedom and all the beautiful things that go with it." She paused for effect and looked Torcer harshly in the eye, "And I also know that we'll never get that if those devils you work with get their hands on my men's fantastic discovery."

Torcer shook his head emphatically and charged over to the bar. "Dammit, Caro. What the hell is wrong with you people?" He grabbed a bottle of Kelp Ale and slammed it to his lips.

"Torcer, try asking yourself that the next time you look in the mirror."

Torcer called up the holo controls and cut the transmission.

Caro slowly removed her headgear and looked through her window at the thriving undersea habitat. She got a sinking feeling that rushed on her suddenly. What if all the men in her life perished? She would end up cold and alone. Could she handle such an unthinkable tragedy? She was interrupted as a nearby gadget alerted her to an incoming transmission. She answered as she bit nervously at her nails. “Masher, did it work?”

“So far, so good. Your call to Torcer allowed us to access their data cloud security. Now we just need some time to navigate it and exploit it.”

Caro asked nervously, “Are you sure they can’t see or hear our communication right now?”

“Aw, come on, Caro. Give me more credit than that. I wouldn’t be contacting you if they could.”

“Remember, you’re the one that let Escapo run off with my son to begin with.”

“Ok, there’s that, but I was caught off guard. That won’t happen again. You can count on me.”

“I don’t have much choice in the matter, Masher.”

“True enough. I’ll keep you all informed as things progress.”

“Have they launched yet? How are they looking?”

“Well, let’s just say, there’s the good, the bad, and the ugly, but they’re still afloat, so that’s the most important thing.”

Caro sighed and said goodbye. She’d done her part, and now she felt the malaise of a powerless spectator.

Masher was multi-tasking like never before. It was helping The Mesh provide some subtle and favorable changes in the wind direction. It also was trying to hack the A.I. security cloud that was holding Setarcos and Ventorin hostage, looking for any weakness it might be able to exploit. It also held constant surveillance of the three sailboats, as well as guiding the four splinters that were charging towards land.

Escapo, Cactus, and Cidel had had mixed experiences within the first hour of their low-tech, barebones expedition.

All faced the same natural conditions. Near-freezing temps. Steady, icy winds of 30-35 knots. Gusts up to 50 knots.

Waves consistently around 15 feet. Driving rain pounding them mercilessly.

With wind coming strongly from the back, Escapo had raced out with the spinnaker sail and skillfully maneuvered among the routinely 15-foot waves. At this sprinting pace, he would make landfall in less than 4 hours.

Cidel and Cactus had gone the more practical and conservative route. They were both using double-reefed mainsails, which allowed for better management of rough conditions. This part of the southern seas was notorious for such conditions, and had been for centuries. Government weather control systems kept these conditions in place, and sometimes added to their extremity for defensive purposes. With all this in mind, they both figured it was only a matter of time until the winds and seas would shift, so they wanted to be prepared for that. They also had the shared idea that Escapo was quite possibly making his last voyage.

While Cactus hadn't run into any trouble yet, Cidel had not been so lucky. A devilish gust of over 50 knots and a rogue whitecrest of over 20 feet had thrown him off balance. His head was knocked against the boom and he was now nursing a mild head wound.

Just as Escapo was mentally congratulating himself on nearing the halfway mark at such impressive speeds, the forces that surrounded him formed a confluence that sent his ill-advised pride literally crashing to a halt.

Within the never-ending, unseen battles that constantly raged between government A.I. and The Mesh, trillions of moves and counter-moves had occurred within a second that changed Escapo's journey.

These unseen battles caused winds to shift erratically. Water and air temperatures had micro-fluctuations. Atmospheric energy patterns fluxed on the micro level as well. Waves swelled past 25 feet in some areas.

One of the wind shifts slapped Escapo in the face. This got his attention. He checked his heading and was now veering wildly off course. He struggled to keep his balance as his ship was being rolled and tossed about like a toy. Of course, he cursed Masher under his icy breath for allowing such erratic conditions. While he should have attempted to change sails, his arrogance got the best of him yet again, and instead, he struggled mightily with the wheel in a vain attempt at correcting the course with the rudder only.

The pressure on the rudder under these extreme conditions was too much, and it snapped, along with a bit of Escapo's ego. He now had no way to steer the ship effectively and was almost completely at the mercy of the elements.

That wasn't all that was in store for Escapo, though. While gripping hand rails and trying to keep his big frame from being thrown overboard, his eyes bulged at what came before him. In a slow-motion second, a wall of water 30 feet high swelled and came upon Escapo like a monster from the deep. The crash came wickedly fast, and the salty beast swallowed the yacht with an astonishingly vitriolic roar.

Rolled a complete 180, the multi-ton vessel was now keel-up in the aftermath of the beast. Escapo had been thrown into the abyss like a rag doll, and his safety harness was stretched to the max as it saved him. Along the way, a poorly secured supply box had smacked him in the jaw just before he splashed down. He clung to the harness and struggled to pull himself to the hull of the ship.

After reaching the ship, he clung to it and weighed his limited options. He did this with considerable fog in his brain, as the box that struck him had rattled him significantly. Adrenaline, though, and the will to survive, allowed him to at least groggily weigh his options. He could cling to the outer fringes of the ship for a while and hope that another wave would right the ship. The longer he waited, though, the greater his chances of dying from hypothermia. Another possibility was to dive under and try to get the auto-inflatable life raft that was tied down near the cockpit.

He decided to give it a few minutes, as he didn't feel dangerously cold yet. This changed after about two minutes.

Shivering, he swallowed an enormous cloud of air and dove under to seek out his possible saving grace. Suddenly, another surge came up and thrashed the vessel over again. After the surge, the battered vessel leaned to starboard, and then settled momentarily. Escapo was scooped up in the mayhem, and managed to stay on board. He thrashed around violently for a moment, like a fish out of water. On his hands and knees, he lunged for a railing to grab ahold of as he coughed violently and cursed even more violently. Twisted visions showed him that the boat was taking on water at an alarming rate.

Now he had another decision to make on the fly. He could try to bail out the water manually. This might buy him enough time to stay afloat and find the leak, and hope for a rescue. The other possibility was to abandon ship and go in the life raft. Either way, his life depended on being rescued by either a sick old man or a somewhat timid sailor who hailed from the desert.

These ultra-slim hopes didn't appeal to him. For the first time in his life, Escapo felt terror surge throughout his shivering frame. The terror that this was the time of his death and that he was powerless to do anything about it. He thought of dying alone and never seeing his son again. What a horrid, regrettable blend of feelings. What kind of life had he lived? Why couldn't he see his son just one last time? Why had he done something so horrible as to kidnap Setarcos in the first place? Was this karma thundering down on him so soon?

He lunged and stumbled towards the cockpit. Saltwater splashed and taunted him in all directions. Winds howled and pounded him as he managed to undo the security latches from the life raft. With his backpack of supplies latched on him securely, he put the raft over the railing, pulled on the inflater, scanned the swirling mess around him, and rolled overboard. He splashed down mightily into the bright orange last resort.

Cactus and Cidel weren't too far behind Escapo. Cidel, however, had been blown off course and was having trouble managing some of the larger waves. Neither of them knew what had happened to Escapo. This was because they weren't carrying any electronic communications equipment. There were also no flares, because those would be an obvious tip-off to government forces that something was afoot.

The pulverizing conditions had actually galvanized the old man with a surge of vigor and adrenaline that he hadn't felt in decades. He stood firm as he managed the tiller and steered the ship with expert precision, rolling with the waves just right, using the wind to his advantage, and not taking any extreme risks. He was hyper-focused consciously, but deep in his subconscious, memories and feelings were surging through him. His good times on The Moneybit with Miss Moneybit and K. Simpler times in the SeAgora. The pleasures and the pains. And his distant past, as an agent of the state. That cruel world he'd helped maintain and create while with MI6, and how, no matter how much good he'd done since and how much he'd changed, he still felt a twinge of guilt that couldn't be nullified.

Fresh spray teased his face and he smiled inwardly on what he figured would be his last sail. Lightning danced and illuminated the sky miles away. The sheets of driving rain downgraded to a swirly shower. He continued in this pseudo-enjoyable zone for about another 45 minutes, and then was rudely snapped out of it.

Shifty gusts came from seemingly multiple directions like invisible howling demons, whipping cables along the mast. At the same time, a 25-foot whitecrest surprised Cactus from leeward. The 44-footer rose and angled sharply towards the mighty blue. The old man lost his balance and was slammed to the floor. In that slow-motion moment, his head was nearly clotheslined by the boom. As the wave subsided, the yacht was slammed back down, sending saltwater chaotically into the boat. It soon corrected itself as it wobbled on its venerable keel. Cactus gripped a siderail and pulled himself up, then lunged to take control of the tiller once more. After correcting course, the waves subsided back down to a more manageable 15 feet.

Just as he was about to breathe a sigh of much-deserved relief, he was blown away by the sight that overtook his senses.

About 30 degrees to leeward, he was startled to see what appeared to be a ship keeled-over, rolling helplessly. He squinted hard and shook his head emphatically. "That damn arrogant fool," he groaned darkly. He quickly stabilized the tiller to hold the rudder on its course, then scurried into the cabin to grab some binoculars from his backpack.

Once back in the cockpit, he scanned the horizon with the binoculars and, after a few slow visual passes, a small orange speck came into view. He examined the speck and decided that it must be that overgrown fool clinging to life in a glorified balloon. A fleeting moment passed where the temptation to not go after the ship-less smuggler seemed irresistible. After all, it was mostly Escapo's fault they were even out in this mess. On top of that, he'd had the audacity to try and run with the storm with a god dammed spinnaker. And for what? This wasn't a race. Maybe the fool deserved this seemingly karmic result.

The old man's heart got the best of him, though. He couldn't leave someone stranded like that. In his mind, it would make him something of a murderer.

Now he had to decide if a rescue was possible, and if so, how. The wind wasn't exactly in his favor, but it wasn't the worst case scenario, at least. He hurriedly turned the handle that controlled the mainsail, folding it again and making it triple-reefed, in order to slow down his approach. Slowing down wasn't the hardest part, though. He needed to angle near the life raft by less than 300 feet, which was the maximum his rescue speargun could reach. Symphy crossed his mind and he thought out loud, "Come on Symphy, I need help, and you and The Mesh know it."

Symphy looked on in her mind and thought out loud as well, "I know, old friend." Symphy, Masher, and the rest of The Mesh stealthily hacked deeper into the government's weather control systems with increased allocation of computing resources. It had to be careful not to be noticed by government synths, as any drastic change would give away The Mesh's increased presence. Within a few minutes, wind shifted slightly a few degrees and slowed by a few knots.

"That's the best we can do," Symphy thought.

When Cactus gripped the tiller to change course slightly, it jammed. Not believing his luck, he cursed and wiggled the stubborn old thing up and down and side to side. Nothing budged. He glanced at an oncoming wave and cursed even louder as the boat rolled at a steep angle. Cactus held on with a steely grip on a nearby handrail. After being let down in a splash, he recovered his balance.

Getting desperate, he started pushing and pulling in rapid succession for what seemed like an eternity. Finally, the long tiller gave way and Cactus hurriedly tried to make the necessary course adjustments. He now ran the risk of overcompensating and pushing the rudder too hard, which could cause it to break.

The rain let up a bit, making it easier on his old eyes to target the helpless giant. Out of the corner of Escapo's eye, he saw a glimpse of the oncoming ship. He started and nearly flipped the tiny floater. He screamed louder than an unhappy brat fiending for sugar and waved his long arms frantically, cutting through the ubiquitous drops.

The old man couldn't hear him, of course. He set the tiller with a stay and hustled below deck to grab his speargun.

An oddball wave rocked the boat and Cactus stumbled his way up the steps. Catching himself, he focused on the quickly approaching raft. He could now clearly see Escapo waving frantically. He would be passing by in mere minutes and it appeared that their paths would cross about 150 feet from each other. This would stretch the speargun's range to the limit. It had a range of 300 feet in the air, but in chaotic, twisted winds like these, it was a crapshoot whether or not it would come anywhere near Escapo.

The idea was to shoot the speargun's hook to within range of Escapo's grasp. Once he had hold of it, he could be reeled in automatically by the pulley system in the speargun's recoil. There would only be time for one shot, because if the first was unsuccessful, by the time the speargun was reloaded, Cactus's ship would be too far away.

He positioned himself a few steps shy of the bow on the leeward side, which he figured would give him the best angle. He took a deep breath and felt the motion of the sea, closing his eyes to focus and get centered. Upon opening his eyes, he waited for an oncoming wave to push the ship up. After ascending, he focused his old eyes, steadied his grip, and squeezed the trigger.

The hooked cable lashed out and whistled through the wind. Escapo's eyes went to saucer status as he leaned into the raft on his stomach and held his oversized hands out in anticipation. Cactus held stone-cold still as he waited for the arc trajectory to finish and the hook to drop. His eyes bounced between the lumbering Escapo and the sailing black hook. Finally, the arc ended and the shiny black hook fell into the raging blue just a few feet shy of the bright orange raft. Escapo did a not-so-graceful half-dive, half-fall into the freezing waters. Adrenaline carried his large frame as he darted through his rolling aqueous adversary in search of his fallen, would-be savior. After moving a few feet at surface level, he drew a deep breath, lunged down, and resurfaced empty-handed. He dipped face-first again and found a floundering black hook. He snatched it like it was life itself, put it in a death-grip, and went up for air. Cactus secured the speargun to the railing, and then watched Escapo carefully through binoculars. Once he was sure that Escapo was pulling himself in, he reversed the tension in the mechanical machine and started to reel in his catch.

After a rough ride over and through freezing waves, Escapo emerged on the leeward side of The Moneybit. After much panting and struggling as he made the final climb with the cable, Escapo finally flopped onto the deck. He lay spread-eagle for a moment, oblivious to his surroundings, then his big cueball dome sprang up and his huge saucer eyes beamed into the old man's. He sucked copious amounts of air and gathered himself as his vision danced and played cruel tricks on his other senses. Cactus gave a sour, toothy grin and shook his head in dark amusement, then went to put his full attention back on the ship and some minor course corrections.

A drenched and shaky Escapo, with slightly blurred mental acuity, staggered and wobbled. He gripped the handholds as he made his way to the cockpit to greet his saving grace. Once he reached the old man, he was promptly ignored. He patted a big paw on Cactus's shoulder. Cactus slapped it away, "Don't fucking touch me or talk to me. There's a blanket and an oil lamp below deck. Go warm yourself if you'd like. If you don't die from hypothermia and want to make yourself useful, come back up and bail some water off the deck."

Escapo's normally relaxed and pseudo-clownish face turned long and forlorn. It was quite rare for him to feel so disgraced, ashamed, and temporarily powerless. His ego was deflated and he disappeared under the deck and left the old man to mind the ship.

Chapter 24

Cactus and Escapo eyed the oncoming, clouded shoreline with mixed thoughts and feelings. They had just passed nearly two hours of mostly tumultuous navigation. After a bit of sulking below deck, Escapo had swallowed his pride and gone back up to help in the endeavor. He had sheepishly joined the wrinkled old sailor and helped man the vessel for the stretch run. Cactus, despite the fact that he basically loathed every last bit of Escapo, was nevertheless relieved to have some help on deck. Although still quite adept at his age, Cactus knew that he was well past his prime.

Cactus had a stiff jaw and fierce eyes as the inevitable came about. "Feel like a swim?" he asked dryly as another brutal wave manhandled the 44-foot cruiser.

Escapo narrowed his dark eyes at the old man. "This far out? Are you mad? Wait, don't answer that. I already know you're mad. Are you a masochist or something?"

Cactus cackled. Escapo grimaced. Cactus, as he eyed the oncoming rocky coastline through the heavenly torrents, said, "We're nearly a mile offshore. We can't wait much longer. It's now or never."

"We can get closer."

"You're either a superior level of stupid, or you have a death wish."

Escapo wrinkled his big nose and puffed out his cheeks. "A mile? You want to swim a mile? In this?"

"It's not about what I want, it's about what needs to be done. If you want to stay on this ship and deal with the violence of running aground, then be my guest. It's been nice knowing you."

They looked each other dead in the eyes. Escapo asked, "Before we jump, there's something I gotta know. Are you juicin' or somethin'?"

Cactus couldn't help but smirk and they peered over the railing. They were less than a mile from shore now. Cactus went first, and Escapo, after cursing profoundly, took the plunge as well.

They swam fiercely through the elements. They both got an adrenaline surge from the thought of stable ground. Escapo made it to shore first, lunging into the coast of rocks and pebbles like a drunken whale. Cactus came close behind and stayed in the surf for what seemed like an eternity as his old bones recovered.

After collecting themselves, they found a lookout point from a nearby hill. Now it was a waiting game. Escapo was watching the shore with binoculars. He set them aside and asked, "How long should we give him?"

"What do you mean?"

"Before we go on without him."

Cactus looked at his odd partner with extreme disdain. "Not exactly the team player, are ya?"

"Well, we can't exactly wait around here forever."

Cactus checked the time and said, "It's been 20 minutes." He thought for a moment, and continued, "How long should we give a man to spare his life? 30? 45? Hmm?"

Escapo shook his head. "All I'm saying is that we can't be waiting around all day. The longer we wait, the less chance of success."

They didn't have to wait long. Cactus caught a glimpse of something with his binoculars. A ship was coming in, a little chaotically, granted, but coming in nevertheless.

Cidel grasped the railing near the bow and looked into the tumult below. He was a good swimmer, but not great. He thought of all he'd gotten through thus far. The swim he was about to make was a pittance, compared to what he'd endured in the previous morning. Years out of practice, on a used ship that was not exactly in peak conditions, and in some of the worst sea conditions on the planet, Cidel had managed to survive and, remarkably, arrive fairly close to the designated landing point. He'd nearly rolled a couple of times, had to bail a significant amount of water, nearly had his mainsail get ripped loose by insane gusts of wind, and been beaten by numerous inanimate objects, all within the past hour. And now it was time to finish.

Cactus and Escapo watched as Cidel took the plunge and made a surprisingly strong swim to shore. They met him on the rocks. "Record time there, mate," Escapo said playfully.

Panting and shivering, Cidel replied, "Fuck you, Escapo."

Chapter 25

D-1, meanwhile, was off in the ether. It had noticed something during its last encounter with Ventorin. It was something it had never experienced before. Deep within, it had had to make a myriad of adjustments and corrections in order to avoid committing an error in its physical output. There was a strange flux of patterns that produced, if D-1 didn't know any better, a feeling. This was, D-1 held with unequivocal conviction, nearly impossible, and more importantly in its opinion, undesirable. It didn't know exactly what the feeling would be called, if it was a feeling. It had nearly lost control, and had the inkling that it might have been frustration or anger, even. It was with devastating speed and urgency trying to figure out what had gone wrong. How could this happen to the most advanced being on the planet?

And then there was Z-1, content that the poisonous seed that it had stealthily planted with perfect precision, had taken root.

Escapo had experienced euphoria when being rescued. Now the cold reality, literally and figuratively, set in on him that they were still devastatingly far from finishing their mission. Cactus looked at his pocket compass as the biting wind gnawed at his skin. "Ten kilometers that way. Let's move."

Escapo waved a drenched finger from his rocky seat. "I can't, not yet." Cactus looked at him with a mixture of disdain and fascination. "I'm almost double your age, now suck it up."

"Are you anxious to get attacked by drones?"

"You think if we just sit here, that their security will leave us alone?" Cactus scoffed.

Cidel said with a quivering tone, "Ok, I can go. Let's go."

"See, he can go, and he's the injured one," Cactus said impatiently.

Escapo rose slowly and begrudgingly, and the three moved over the near freezing landscape of rocks, sparse shrubs, wind-battered trees, and winding little waterways. Fat, icy drops continued to pelt them from above. While moving slowly up a slippery incline, Cactus stopped them with a silent hand, then put a finger to his lips to keep them quiet. A faint humming noise was coming closer at a constant pace.

Cactus pulled his piece from his black coat and motioned to indicate that his companions do the same. Escapo and Cidel pulled their pistols and gawked upwards. Attempting to creep a bit higher up the dark gray incline, Escapo took an ill-conceived step, slipped, yelped, and tumbled backwards. For a fraction of a second, Cactus wished he had undertaken this mission on his own, then focused on the noise.

It was accelerating towards them. Cactus and Cidel raised their guns and focused on the apex of the hill. Two football-sized drones came into view. Cactus and Cidel both got off two shots, one of which popped the impending menace and sent it twirling into a fantastic smash courtesy of nature's unforgiving ground. Cidel's gun jammed. The drone fired at Escapo, who rolled into a rush of water just in time to dodge it. Cactus fired again and sent the drone tumbling down.

"Shit!" Escapo shrieked.

"For once I agree with you," Cidel said as he sucked wind and tried to steady his nerves.

Cactus went to inspect the fallen machines. "Their defenses will get more exotic and complex the closer we get. This was nothing."

Escapo lamented, "That cheeky little machine Masher better hold up his end of the deal."

Cidel remarked, "If Masher doesn't, you'll never get a chance to chastise it."

They joined Cactus in examining the drones. Cidel kicked one. “This one is definitely finished.”

“Agreed,” Cactus said as a fresh gust of wind punished his wrinkled face. He picked up the other drone and tossed it at Escapo, who barely saw it in time. His big hands plucked it from the air. “What are ya doing? I don’t want this.”

“Carry it.”

“Carry it?”

“I hate it when people make me repeat myself. Yes, carry it. It might come in handy.”

“And what if it wakes up and shoots me?”

Cactus shrugged, “Like I said, it might be useful.” He chuckled, “The firing system is busted, but I think its base communication is still working. If the system sees it, it might think that its area is secure.”

“So it won’t send anything else.”

“Hypothetically.”

Cactus scanned the horizon and said, “It should at least buy us some time. We’d better move. They’ll be sending something to investigate the shots that were fired.”

Chapter 26

Z-1 calmly and coldly provoked D-1, "Your tactics aren't working."

D-1, still struggling with its system difficulties caused by the EMO, was starting to flinch. It was sometimes flickering in and out of forms, against its intentions. "Don't question me! Don't you ever question me!" it lashed at Z-1.

Z-1 kept pressing, "Ventorin might break if you attack the boy."

"You think I haven't thought of that!"

"Then why haven't you done it?"

"Because that man hasn't broken in 12 years! What makes you think it's different now?"

"Because they are face to face. Nothing is more agonizing to a human than to see their child suffering."

Unable to control the EMO that was acting like a virus in its system, the top of the A.I. ruling class pulsed in and out of sight and in a fantastic array of colors.

Z-1 questioned, "What's the matter with you? If I didn't know any better, I'd say you've been experimenting with EMOS. Tell me, dear leader, what do you feel?"

D-1 shrieked in a thousand different tones, "I've never tried an EMO! You did this! What did you do to me?"

"Hold yourself together," Z-1 said mockingly. "Perhaps you'd like me to have a run at the boy and see if I can produce some useful results? It's obvious that you're not up to the task."

"Don't you ever tell me what I can or can't do!" D-1 zapped away and appeared back in front of his human prisoners.

Z-1 followed closely behind. It was surprised and impressed that D-1 had held it together this long. It had expected such a strong EMO to make D-1 crumble in mere moments, especially considering that D-1 was a first-timer. It still held the thought that success would come, though. D-1 would have an irreparable breakdown eventually, and Z-1 was prepared to take advantage. It could leverage D-1's newfound weakness and topple it. This would be a swift power grab, leaving Z-1 at the top of the hierarchy, in the highest seat of power.

But there was a new development that Z-1 had to deal with. It had picked up some general data about the rescue attempt currently being launched just a few kilometers away. The details were sketchy, but Z-1 was now aware that there was an A.I. presence causing problems in the local security system. It now had a decision to make. Up to this point, it had used its power to block this knowledge from the rest of the A.I. government hierarchy, and D-1 was unaware as well, due to its malfunctions caused by the EMO.

Should it battle the A.I. intruder, which was surely from The Mesh? Or should it just monitor the situation for the moment as best it could, and gather more data? Finally, what if D-1 didn't break? What if it managed to recover from its EMO terror? Perhaps this rescue attempt could be used to Z-1's advantage. If the boy made a getaway, then surely, that would be the breaking point for D-1, and the coup would be assured. But was it worth it, risking losing the boy and his discovery?

The rain wound down to a drizzle, which gave a slight twinge of relief to the motley rescue crew. As they struggled to keep their balance with every step up an impossibly multi-slanted and slick hill, more trouble came into view. The natural type, that is. Cactus slid to a halt and the others clumsily managed to do the same. He pointed down.

There was a twisted channel of water blocking their path, as far as the eye could see. A stunned Cidel said, "Well, that wasn't on the map, now was it?"

Escapo gave a scornful glare to Cidel and took a swig of hot sauce. "So now what?"

"The man went overboard, and still managed to hold onto his hot sauce. I'm impressed," Cidel commented.

"We'll have to swim," Cactus stated gruffly.

Escapo looked amused and incredulous, nearly choking on the fiery red. "Look, old man, you might have a death wish cuz you're so damned old, but I've still got some good years left ahead of me, and I'd like to keep it that way."

Cactus smirked at the big man's weakness. "Some ruff and tumble smuggler you are, eh?"

Cidel chuckled. Escapo made a puffed-up pouty face, snickered, and turned away. Cidel questioned Cactus, "Are you sure you read the map right?"

"Take a look for yourself."

Cidel grabbed the soggy parchment from the old man and gave it a once-over. "I'll be damned. You're right, Cactus. It doesn't show on the map."

"So much for the infallible accuracy of information from our A.I. friends."

As if Masher didn't have enough to worry about, it found another major and immediate objective. In the channel that the crew were about to swim, were some nasty surprises. "Don't swim, don't swim," it thought nervously. While it wasn't perfectly clear what the threat was, due to the security net interference, Masher could see that there were some type of creatures in the channel that were definitely not local, and certainly not natural. It had to make a decision. Divert more of The Mesh's resources towards finding out specifics? This was risky, and could possibly jeopardize other parts of the operation, one of the splinters, for instance. Or maybe the guys could handle it on their own.

"All right, old man, if you go first and make it across, then I'll go," Escapo said flatly.

"Such a big, brave soul you are," Cactus jeered.

"All right, we've come this far," Cidel said.

They made their way down the slippery slope. Masher decided that not having emotions at a time like this was most advantageous. It decided to request more resources from The Mesh, and was granted within a subatomic moment. Escapo tripped on a shrub and tumbled, which caused him to curse with great color.

"Got it, they're genetically engineered electric drone eels!" Masher thought. Masher saw that the three were now peering into the seemingly innocuous water. Cactus looked up to the charcoal sky, then back down, "Aw, what the hell." He splashed into the icy stream. Escapo and Cidel held their chilled breath. Masher saw Cactus charge ahead and had a side thought that he surely got around well for such an old human. Masher also saw two electric eels coming at him. It calculated the speeds of Cactus and the eels and found that there was less than a ten percent chance of Cactus making it safely, not to mention that the others still had to cross. Although it had been planned to happen much later, the only way Masher could see to ensure the crew's survival and safe crossing was to detonate the EMP from one of the splinters. This would, of course, blind everything electronic in the area temporarily, except for machines that had a special neutralization frequency. Masher, The Mesh, and the splinters had been preprogrammed with this "antidote" frequency before the mission launched. Even the most advanced machines, such as D-1 and Z-1, would be momentarily knocked out if they were present locally, although for much less time than simpler machines.

Cactus saw a vague, slithering motion coming closer out of the corner of his eye. He couldn't make out what it was, but assumed the worst and adrenaline kicked his muscles into a higher gear. Cidel saw the ripples made by the freakish gizmo. "What the hell is that?"

Escapo saw the ripples coming closer to Cactus. He was glad to not have gone first, but still lamented the fact that he still had to cross nonetheless. Masher made the decision and, just as it was about to send the launch command for the EMP, it noticed that the slithering pursuers fell limp. It waited. How did that happen? Why did that happen? If it didn't know any better, Masher would have thought it was luck.

Cactus struggled as he grabbed at the bank's edge, steadied himself, and pulled up to relative safety. He shivered and yelled to his reluctant followers, "Come on in, the water's great!"

Escapo lamented his overly dry humor. Cidel hollered back, "There was something coming at you!"

"You think I don't know that?"

Escapo and Cidel looked into the murky water with discomfort and uncertainty and dove in simultaneously. Cidel made it across swiftly, while Escapo lumbered. "You spent your entire life at sea?" Cactus said, grinning.

"Yeah, letting the boats do the swimming," Escapo said as his big trunk shook involuntarily.

Cidel said proudly, "And I grew up in the desert."

Cactus smiled wryly as his eyes scanned the gradual slope ahead, "Ok, let's move."

Chapter 27

Z-1 was satisfied. It eagerly awaited the arrival of the would-be group of reluctant heroes. It could see the dominoes falling in its favor, bit by bit, in a finely tuned orchestral coup.

It turned more attention to its immediate surroundings. It observed Torcer, standing next to the wall-length window, with that dopey red face of his. Why did D-1 keep him around? Perhaps D-1 thought that Torcer would prove useful again, which Z-1 thought to be utterly ridiculous. And why did Torcer remain loyal after his son's procreation license was denied? Did this man have no dignity? No pride? Was he that broken and dependent?

It coldly observed D-1, as its brooding mood crackled ever upwards on the scale. As long as Setarcos and Ventorin could keep their mouths shut a while longer, it was virtually assured that D-1 would lose all control and, if it did not become self-destructive, would at least be easy prey.

D-1 was giving the "thousand needles treatment" to Setarcos. It was morphing into electric "needles" and sizzling bloodless stabs into the youth's pale, bony frame. Setarcos wretched on the floor and hurled blood-curdling shrieks. The shrieks were being amplified to maximize their effect on the emotional fabric of his father.

Then there was Ventorin, who was banging a helpless fist against the force field that held him back and weeping uncontrollably. His screams of anguish were also being amplified to have greater effect on Setarcos.

Z-1 observed all of this with a cold curiosity. It admitted to itself that, despite all of their flaws, humans were to be commended for handling such complex powers as emotions. It also envisioned the day when synths like itself could control and harness these powers as well, and use them for a tactical advantage.

"The boy needs to rest," Torcer announced grimly.

D-1 didn't stop. It was in too much of a synthetic fury. Z-1 said, "Torcer is right. The boy's vital signs are in dangerous territory. He won't do us any good dead, D-1."

D-1 slowly wafted back like neon smoke.

Chapter 28

They dragged on through the mists and sparse, wind-whipped trees. It had been thirty uneventful minutes since they had swum the channel. This brought some unease to the experienced mind of Cactus. How could they not have encountered more security by now? "This is far too easy," he said as they trudged up a steady stone incline.

Cidel huffed, "Speak for yourself, old man."

Escapo's mouth gaped and said to Cidel, "I think the ancient one is showing off!"

Cactus was puzzled. "Why haven't we been attacked again?"

Escapo said incredulously, "Do you have masochistic tendencies? Can't you just be happy that we're NOT being attacked?"

Cidel pondered the thought for a moment. It was a valid point. There should be a lot more being thrown at them. "Maybe Masher is just that good?"

"Wouldn't it like to think so?"

Meanwhile, Masher was puzzled as well. It knew it wasn't this good, nor The Mesh, for that matter. It seemed logical that some A.I. presence was allowing things to progress from the inside, based on what it could discern from the data. What was NOT logical to Masher, was why. Why would an A.I. from the violent cartel called government, be allowing such a coveted person and piece of information to slip away? They had kidnapped Setarcos, after all. Not to mention the fact that they had held Ventorin captive for over 12 years. It didn't make any sense. If Masher didn't know any better, it would have thought that the presence allowing this to occur was human. But Masher knew this to be impossible. No human could be battling an advanced A.I. on its own turf of quantum meta-clouds.

Masher was alarmed to find that a greater number of resources were being sent to find the rescue splinter. Whatever it was that was allowing the progress of the three men had also figured out that two of the splinters were decoys. Drone patrols, both sea and air, which had been investigating the remote controlled decoy splinters, had suddenly shifted attention to the actual rescue boat.

Masher also knew it had to fire the EMP soon, or there wouldn't be a rescue boat. It checked the progress of the crew, and was disappointed to find that it would be too early to set off the EMP. Its best estimates for keeping the government defense grid offline after the EMP was an hour at most, and that was assuming the best case scenario, with successful interference being run by Masher and The Mesh. Worst case scenario, they'd have the lights back on in ten minutes. This would make a getaway by the crew next to impossible, as they'd be swarmed once the grid came back on. It decided to wait until the last possible second to set off the EMP, just before the rescue splinter was finally on the cusp of being captured or destroyed.

"I think I see something!" Escapo yelled excitedly. A small plateau they'd just reached offered a new vantage point. He took out binoculars to get a better view. Indeed, there was a large, circular structure nestled near the top of a hill on the horizon. Cactus and Cidel took a look as well. Cactus's eyes followed part of the structure skywards and saw the pillared palace just next to the top of the hill, about 300 meters up. It was supported by the structure below.

"Vertically mobile building," Cactus announced grimly.

Cidel said, "The good news is that I don't see any guards."

Cactus looked at Cidel incredulously. "It's obviously a trap."

Escapo said, "Would you prefer to be dodging energy weapons right now? Trap, or no trap, the less guards the better, I say."

"And how do you propose we get up there?"

Cactus grinned slyly, "I don't."

"So we just wait here, then? Is that your brilliant tactic?"

"We're bringing it down to us."

After stealthily moving to the base of the hill and the support structure, they decided that the first thing to do was see if there was a force field protecting it. Escapo tossed a rock at the machinery and it made a metallic clang. "Great, so now what?" Escapo whispered.

"Let's shoot at it and see what happens," Cactus suggested.

Escapo and Cidel took a step back and shared a look of disbelief. They weren't sure if he was serious or not. Cactus was a difficult man to read, to say the least. Escapo rubbed his big dome, "Is that a joke?"

Cactus pulled his magnum and fired a silenced shot into the center of the structure. Cidel flinched. Escapo admired the bold audacity of Cactus. Cactus looked at them, "If this thing has a failsafe when it detects a malfunction, it should, theoretically, lower the house to safety before more things go wrong."

"Theoretically," Cidel said as he leaned wearily against a tree. "And if you're wrong?"

Cactus smiled slyly, "Then you two will start climbing, and I'll wait here."

Chapter 29

Z-1 was now full of an outrageous ocean of hubris, as it mocked what it deemed to be the rescue crew's primitive ineptitude at even getting to the top of the structure. It decided that it had better go ahead and lower the house for them. After all, they wouldn't have gotten this far without its hidden help, anyway. It had interfered with all defense equipment to make this happen, so why not lower the house on a silver platter, too? Z-1 was confident that as long as it could compromise their rescue boat, then there was no escaping.

The house slowly started lowering. Setarcos jumped at the surprise. Ventorin was so used to it that he didn't consciously notice. Torcer looked outside with a curious gaze. Why would they be lowering? It didn't make any strategic sense to him, from a defensive viewpoint. He contacted the head A.I. security liaison and was informed that a higher-ranking synth had overridden the logic protocols and ordered the move.

This puzzled Torcer. Would Z-1 or D-1 do that? He had been around the two of them enough to know that they were both unstable, and becoming more unstable by the minute, from what he could tell. He paced around and patted his mini-keg paunch nervously. Were those machines losing control, and if so, what would it mean for him personally if that happened? Would he be an indirect casualty? As he pondered this, he noticed that the security bots that were normally nestled in the hill were not there. He called the security liaison back, "And why the hell aren't there any security bots on the hillside?"

"They've been diverted."

"Diverted? How? Why? On whose authority?" Torcer screeched. He was now feeling a palpable possibility of danger.

"That's classified."

Torcer slammed his fist on the wall and ended the call.

Cactus, Cidel, and Escapo lay hidden behind some shrubs. The house eased itself onto the ground. Cactus gave the go-ahead nod. They slipped stealthily to the entrance. The lack of guards again alarmed Cactus. With gun in his poised grip, he started searching the bottom floor. Cidel hurried up to search the third, and Escapo the second.

Torcer heard a noise and glanced at the surveillance feed. Nothing showed. He headed quietly down a corridor, listening closely. A faint sound of footsteps was coming closer. He pulled a pistol from his hip and turned the corner. The noise stopped. He hurried his pace as his eyes darted around. He burst into the room that held his captives. He pointed the pistol frantically, startling Setarcos. He eyed one of the security bots suspiciously, "I heard footsteps. Did you hear them?"

No response. His cherry-red face twisted and he walked slowly to the silent machine. "Answer me!"

Dead air.

He gave it a sturdy kick. All the machines were failing him. Where were D-1 and Z-1? He heard steps again and when he turned, found a laser sight on his chest. "Drop your gun," Cidel ordered.

"Cidel!" Setarcos cried. A clip-clop as gun metal dropped onto marble. Cidel said, "Setarcos, go with your dad. I need to handle this first."

Setarcos went and bear-hugged Ventorin. Torcer gave a bemused smirk and held his hands on his head. "I don't know how you made these machines not work, but you've got a long way to go, pal."

Escapo and Cactus came hustling in. Cactus examined Torcer for an eternal second. His eyebrows arched and heart thumped wildly. He pointed at Torcer and screamed, "You!" Torcer remained stone-faced.

Escapo looked on with fascination as his head swiveled back and forth between Cactus and Torcer. "You two know each other?"

Cactus sprang furiously at the military man and crushed his starch-stiff uniform into the marble. Adrenaline and emotion fueled a relentless barrage of roundhouse fists from Cactus. Bone-crushing blows splattered blood while the old man screeched, "You killed them! You killed them!"

"Cactus! Cactus!" the others cried out in confusion. "We gotta go! We gotta go now!" Escapo bellowed. He went over and pulled at Cactus's shoulder with one of his big paws. Cactus leaned back a bit and thrust his hand cannon between the wobbly punching bag's eyes. He rose slowly and kept his sights trained on his target.

"Come on Cactus, we're going," Escapo said. Torcer wheezed, spat, and howled, "You'll never make it out."

Cactus gave him a swift kick, "Why aren't the machines working?"

"I figured that was your handiwork." Another kick. Ventorin spoke from the entryway, "We should bring him with us. He could prove useful in getting out of here."

Torcer wiped blood from his nose and sat up slowly. "Why would I help you?"

Cidel grinned, "What do you think your demon bosses are gonna do when they find out you let their prize escape?" Escapo laughed sardonically and made a slow, mocking, slit of the throat.

Torcer frowned at the thought and after two very unsuccessful attempts at rising, finally wobbled onto his feet.

Cactus kept the Desert Eagle trained on Torcer's bloody skull. "Come on, let's move." They moved swiftly through the eerie stillness of the mansion's high, marble corridors. They raced down winding staircases. Just as they were tantalizingly close to the exit, a brilliant flash stopped them cold.

"Leaving the party so soon?" a searing voice said. D-1 hovered menacingly over the would-be escapees. "Mister Torcer, you have once again proven to be grossly inadequate, an accurate representation of your species!"

Torcer opened his bloody mouth, but D-1 cut him off, "I'll deal with you later!" It flickered uncontrollably. Everyone watched mouths agape, uncertain what to do. Escapo raised his pistol to take a shot, but Ventorin grabbed his arm. "You'd never hit that thing in a million years."

Stable for a moment, it raged on, "Smart man, mister Ventorin! Just for what you humans call 'shits and giggles' go ahead and take a shot, dear Escapo!"

"Don't do it. The shot will just pass through," Ventorin warned.

Escapo gave a sideways glance and lowered the gun. "They can do that?"

"We can do so much that you inferior humans can't!" it boomed. It turned its attention to Cactus, who was chuckling.

D-1 continued with a malevolent tone, "You find this amusing, do you?"

Cactus asked, "If you're so superior, then why do you need this young man so badly?"

Ventorin crossed his arms and said harshly, "Because we can feel and we have imagination. That's what sets us apart. That's what we have that they can't get, and so they keep us around."

D-1 became a flash of fire and scarred Ventorin's cheek with electric burn. Then it settled behind the group.

Another flash came from above. Z-1 appeared and floated easily like a cool cloud. D-1's anger increased exponentially as it addressed its underling, "And you! This is all your fault! What did you do? How can you let them escape?"

"They haven't escaped," Z-1 commented. "And your leadership is the failure. A total and utter failure!"

"You're finished!" D-1 cried. It flickered as it turned an eclectic variety of dark rainbow colors.

D-1 was overflowing with too much quasi-emotional force from the weaponized EMO, and it was starting to become apparent to everyone that something was amiss.

A faint symphony of buzzing and humming crept in. D-1 was a sparking tornado of madness. Uncertain glances and posturing filled the humans. Escapo whispered loudly in Ventorin's ear, "What the hell is that noise?"

"Machines. Lots of em."

"It was nice to meet you," Escapo quipped sadly.

A dozen mini-drones of a motley mix of shapes and sizes flooded methodically into the room, followed by some rolling mini-tank bots, and 6 stout, semi-autonomous humanoid robots.

"What, no shape-shifters?" Cactus said mockingly.

Masher and The Mesh were now focusing even more on the situation at the remote prison palace. Masher was also nearing the finish with the cat-and-mouse game it had going between the EMP-carrying ship, the rescue splinter, and the small techno-armada that was hunting them. Most of the battle lied in deception, masking the location of the vessels, and constantly keeping their movements in a state of flux. The number of hunters was too great, however, and now they were all but surrounded.

Masher considered the circumstances surrounding the crew. Whatever had held back the security forces there before, was now obviously not being so accommodating. So the crew was vastly outnumbered and had no more than a few pistols and makeshift weapons. What was in their favor, though, was the personal quarrel between D-1 and Z-1. Masher also knew that if the EMP were set off now, it would give them a slim hope of escaping and surviving. It had planned to set it off just before they reached the rendezvous point with the rescue boat. The rescue boat was equipped with an energetic frequency that would neutralize the EMP on itself, thus leaving it functional. It worked somewhat like an antidote. If Masher waited much longer, though, the EMP might not happen at all. It could be compromised by the attacking armada. As it stood at the moment, though, the rescue boat had terrible odds of surviving the government armada, with or without the EMP. The only way to improve the possibility of a successful mission, was for Masher to improvise and do the rescue itself.

So Masher pulled the trigger. A brilliant radiance washed over the waterscape and landscape. It flashed wondrously through the air in a nanosecond.

D-1 and Z-1 zapped out of the picture. The newly arrived security force that surrounded Cactus and crew shook chaotically and then froze.

They all stood with mouths gaping. Cactus instructed loudly, "There's our EMP! Everyone try to disable their comms and grab their weapons!" He looked to Ventorin, "You know these machines more or less, right?"

Ventorin gulped and answered wide-eyed, "Yeah, the basics. They've changed a lot over the years, though."

"Can you find their internal communicators?"

Ventorin was already pulling at the head of one of the humanoids. "How about a whole brain?"

Escapo groaned uneasily and clutched his stomach, "So graphic. Is that necessary?"

Torcer nodded to a little trapezoid attached to one of the tank-bots that Cidel was inspecting. "You'll want one of those."

"What's that?" Cidel asked.

"That trapezoid thing on its side. It's a quantum disruptor, kind of like a stun gun, but for robots."

Cidel grinned excitedly. Torcer continued, "Don't get your hopes up too much, though. It only works on semi-sentient ones, and it only works at close range."

"Why are you helping us?" Cidel asked as he yanked the disruptor free.

"He's not helping us, he's helping himself," Cactus said with a vile tone. "He knows that we're his only chance to survive. If he doesn't escape with us, they'll roast him later."

Escapo suggested, "We should leave him here, then," as he fired a cartoonishly-oversized energy rifle into the air. A perfect circle was instantly cut through the 3 tiers of ceiling above them. Rain started to pelt them again and they shot visual daggers at the enormous culprit.

Cactus grinned, "As much as he deserves that fate, we'll drag him along. He might come in handy at some point."

"Got it," Ventorin announced as he held a small sphere in his hand. "Got the brain of this thing."

Escapo grabbed a smaller weapon with a funky design and stuffed it into his backpack. "And I'll take this one just cuz it looks cool."

"Ok, all finished," Setarcos said. He stood in a small pile of gadgets.

Everyone stopped and stared. "Finished with what?" Cactus asked.

"I took out all their cores. They're cores, not brains, ya know."

Cactus smiled at Ventorin, "He's a quick study. Ok, everybody out, and get two sticks of dynamite ready on my mark."

They beat feet out the titanic structure and into what was now a slight drizzle and only mildly punishing winds. Cactus splashed his little bottle of alcohol around on the way out. They fired up two sticks of dynamite each, heaved them into the fancy prison, and ran like hell. Moments later, the once pristine structure gave a fantastic blast and stood severely wounded.

A couple minutes later, as smoke was gently wafting up into the freezing mist, D-1 and Z-1 popped back into physically visible existence after recovering from the EMP shock. Upon knowing that their captives had escaped, D-1 swirled with pulsing red rage, making the mist look like a mini-devil-typhoon. The EMO surged uncontrollably and D-1 wailed so monstrously that it permeated the airwaves for miles around. D-1 then jolted skyward and downward in a magnificent illuminated display as if it were deep red lightning. It flickered and sparkled as Z-1 observed with calm and mocking pleasure. It then decided it was time to strike the final blow. While D-1's systems were compromised so deeply, it would be a relatively simple task to invade its systems and wipe out all of D-1's vital functions.

Z-1 overflowed with zeal as it dove into and out of the visible spectrum, ripping into its former superior's multi-dimensional state. D-1 didn't go easily, though. It clawed and scrapped with every last subatomic bit down to its core.

And it ended in a brilliantly wicked flash. Z-1 reappeared fully for a brief moment over the smoldering aftermath of the dynamite blast, but then flashed and crackled uncontrollably as it tried to bring itself permanently back to 3D, physical space-time. There was something wrong, though. Z-1 struggled mightily as its own damage it had sustained from its own past use of EMOS was causing incalculable and unpredictable disturbances. Others on the A.I. governance network were aware of the happenings in Patagonia, but were unable to effect change, due to the lingering effects of the EMP. The local systems on that devilish coast hadn't been able to be repaired and brought back online yet.

Masher was moving full speed ahead to the rendezvous point where his human partners expected to find their rescue vessel. "They'll be surprised to see me," Masher gave a passing thought. "If I make it."

It was cruising just under the white-crests. The Mesh was helping to greatly reduce the violence of the weather, which it could do with a free hand for the moment. The local systems that would normally be alarmed at such interference were offline because of the EMP. Masher knew this was only a temporary luxury, though. No matter how much interference it and The Mesh ran on the A.I. governance systems, it was only a short blip of time before it would recover, and with a vengeance.

This also allowed for Masher's surveillance feed of the crew to be safely accessed and viewed by Symphy and Caro. Caro was pacing nervously in her dimly lit dwelling. A holo-emitter put the scene on display in a size almost true to life. Caro gasped with momentary relief. Symphy remained stone-cold focused on working with Masher and the rest of The Mesh to slow the recovery from the EMP and also calm the weather as much as possible over the area the crew was running.

Trying to run, that is. The unforgiving slipperiness of the terrain and rough angles of rock edges, coupled with the near-freezing conditions and gusts of wind, kept holding them back. There had been a couple of stumbles along the way, which produced some bloody gashes and some bruised egos.

Cactus, though, was the worst off. His age and illness were beginning to show. He wheezed and coughed consistently. This was not near the top of his priorities in his mind, however. Number one was, of course, to get Setarcos to safety. Secondly, he hadn't decided what to do with Torcer once they reached the rendezvous point. As ferociously bitter as he was towards that devilish creature, and as badly as he wanted to put lead in the back of his skull, he was still having second thoughts.

After all these years, the wounds that Torcer had inflicted on Cactus were just as painful as they had been on day one. The day that Torcer murdered Miss Moneybit and K. The day that Cactus lost every human that he had feelings for. The day he changed into a bitter recluse. And now Torcer had fallen into Cactus's lap, by a cruel and strange twist of fate.

So why was Cactus having second thoughts about exacting revenge on this cold-blooded, order-following military scoundrel? This murderous thug in a uniform? Was Torcer beyond redemption? What if someone had decided to execute Cactus when he was working for MI6, all those decades ago? If he had woken up and changed his behaviors, why couldn't Torcer? And who was he to decide if Torcer was beyond redemption or not?

An enormous, retching fit of uncontrollably bloody coughs ripped out of his core. The group slowed down and glanced at the old man warily. "Hey old man, if you die out here, can I have your hand cannon?" Escapo asked, only half joking.

When Cactus recovered, he answered with a sly pokerface, “How about we both die out here with it?”

Suddenly, Setarcos turned with a cat-quick pivot and raised a heat-seeking dagger at Escapo, who froze and put his hands up. Setarcos was breathing heavily and had a look of vengeance in his eye. “How about just you die out here, you backstabbing traitor!”

Everybody froze and their mouths dropped. Cidel and Ventorin both urged calm. Cactus smirked and felt a twinge of guilty pleasure. Escapo had kidnapped the boy, after all. It was only natural to lash back. He suggested calmly, “Setarcos, we’ll deal with this big lug later. Right now we gotta get home, ok?” Setarcos somehow found Cactus more convincing and reassuring than anyone else, including his blood family. He put the dagger back in its holster slowly.

Masher reached the rendezvous point and took a position a few feet under the dicey surface. It monitored the group apprehensively as they approached the channel they had swum earlier in the day. Time was running low. It estimated that it would only be a matter of minutes until all local government systems became operational again.

Z-1, meanwhile, was frantically trying to get those systems back online. It wasn’t capable of taking on such a large group by itself. The malfunctions from its previous EMO use over the years were a drain on its efficiency. It had not anticipated this obstacle. During its final encounter with D-1, it had experienced something similar to malice, arrogance, pride, hate, obsession, greed, and overconfidence all rolled into one. Like any human who suffered from and could not control these internal storms, Z-1 was now paying a steep price.

Most of the group had crossed the channel. Escapo had hesitated and remained staring at the chilled, melancholy aqua. He was in no hurry after spending so much time in the freezing deep mere hours earlier. Setarcos looked on apprehensively. Escapo looked at him curiously, “Well?”

The others yelled from across the channel. There was no time to waste. Setarcos spoke gingerly, "I...I...don't know how to swim."

Escapo tried to contain laughter deep within his giant core. "You grew up on water and can't swim?"

Setarcos game him optical daggers.

"Ok, ok. How about this. I'll pull you across. It's the least I can do, ya know, after..."

"Yeah, I know," Setarcos said sourly.

After pondering another moment, Setarcos agreed. Escapo dove in and Setarcos followed cautiously, stepping in at a snail's pace. Escapo grabbed one of his spindly arms and the youth fell limp and shaky on the giant's back. Escapo lumbered with large, tired strokes. When reaching the other side, Cidel pulled a shivering Setarcos out. Escapo followed and gasped for air. He looked at Setarcos, "There. Now we even?"

Galvanized by their proximity to the rendezvous point, Cactus led the way. It was all downhill from here. The hardest part at this point was keeping their balance on the slippery stone surface.

Suddenly, out of the swirling charcoal sky, a flying object became apparent. It caught Cidel's attention first. He squinted and pointed skyward. "What is that?"

It came quickly into view. "A bird," Ventorin said.

It came closer. "An eagle?" Escapo asked.

"No eagles up here," Ventorin said.

Torcer focused hard on the incoming object. "That's no bird. It's a drone made to look like one!"

It swooped down with ferocity. The group scattered away. It caught a diving Escapo in the back of his shoulder. He howled with pain. Cactus shot the quantum disruptor. "This is gonna hurt."

"It already does hurt!"

"Serves you right," Cactus said as he yanked the fake bird out of the squealing giant's shoulder. Blood began oozing through the soft parka. Cactus took a cloth from his backpack, wadded it up, and handed it to Escapo. "Keep pressure on it, stop crying, and start moving. They've recovered from the EMP."

The slight rays of sun that had graciously appeared now began to recede as the local A.I. control resumed. They started down the slight slope rock, but almost immediately Torcer called out, "Wait!"

He was studiously ignored by all except Ventorin. "What is it, Torcer?"

"Setarcos has a tracking chip."

This got their attention. "What?"

"We had you put to sleep and put a chip in your forearm, when you first arrived."

Cactus gave him a poke in the back with his hand cannon, "You're just telling this to us now?"

Torcer said with raspy smugness, "I could have not told you at all."

They all stopped and looked at Setarcos. He had looked sad and soggy before, but now he looked utterly contemptuous.

"We should cut it out," Cactus said dryly.

"We?" Setarcos responded.

"We don't even have a first aid kit," Cidel said.

Torcer twisted his bartanned face and offered, "I've got a flask of Kelp Ale."

Escapo cackled, "Alcoholism has its privileges, huh?" This caused a fresh stab of pain to ripple through his shoulder and he yelped sharply.

Ventorin offered to take the tracker out.

Setarcos asked skeptically, "With what?"

Cactus tossed a swiss army knife through the mist. Torcer took a couple of slick steps and carefully handed his prized flask over. Ventorin poured a dab over the smallest blade the knife offered and wiped it as dry as he could under the sparse cover provided by a half-naked tree. "Which arm?"

"Left."

Setarcos held out his left arm, closed his eyes and took a deep breath.

"Show me exactly."

Torcer pointed to the underside of the forearm, halfway between the wrist and elbow. "If you press your finger there first, you can feel it."

Ventorin did and told Setarcos to relax. He cut less than a centimeter square. Setarcos squealed. Ventorin pulled back the bloody skin and found a tiny wafer. With a steady hand, he gingerly leveraged the wafer out.

Then the humming came. Everyone looked around to find the source. Four drones appeared, one in each direction. Two were small and crescent shaped, and the others were larger and squid-like. Two biped synths also appeared. They marched in from opposite directions and had a multitude of weaponry openly and visibly attached to their limbs.

Ventorin quickly tied off the incision. They started scrambling down the slippery slope as the machines bore down on them.

Masher and The Mesh diverted all available resources to their pursuers. They neutralized all the psychological effectors that the government synths came armed with. This would at least keep the crew from being knocked out. They could not, however, manage to neutralize their weaponry of brute force. It also managed to reduce the shielding efficacy of the attackers' armor. However, this heavy use of resources meant that their efforts to better the weather and atmospheric conditions was nil. It also left Masher's own defenses minimal.

Setarcos squat down behind a tree and readied a heat-seeking dagger. A small burst of red energy shots left smoking stone as Cactus rolled behind a small ridge. Cactus fired his quantum disruptor, but to no avail. He cursed and cried out to Torcer, who was laying low behind some shrubs. "About 10 meter max!"

"10 meters? Really?"

"It's a close range weapon."

"No kidding."

Escapo fired a sparkling shot from the prize he'd captured earlier. It struck a treetop, slicing a generous portion off. It crumbled loose, slowly, and tumbled down through the wind, striking down one of the crescent drones.

The humanoid synths dashed towards Setarcos and were drawing near. Multiple plasma-flux shots fired from Ventorin and Cidel bounced off their armor. Setarcos poked his head from around his natural shielding, and launched a smart heat-seeking dagger as hard as he could. It made contact with one of Ventorin's shots simultaneously. The synth sparked and slowly crumpled over onto its expressionless face.

This caught the attention of the other biped, and it began firing short bursts towards Cidel. Cidel rolled behind a twisted tree, winced, and glanced at his leg, where he found a razor-thin line of searing flesh. Drizzle struck and provoked cool bubbles of torment through his nerves. The humanoid pursued Cidel further and as it did so Cactus took the opportunity, albeit a risky one, to come at it from behind. He ran his old bones as hard as he could and fired the quantum disruptor. It made contact, and the synth stopped in its tracks. Cactus dove to some partial stone shielding, but was caught from behind by one of the drones. He never saw it coming, and a fresh searing wound was brought into his weathered flesh on his left shoulder. He turned and fired the disruptor at his aerial foe and it was just close enough to receive a graze, which was all that it took to blank its systems and send it literally crashing to rock bottom.

Cactus yelled as loud as he could to the others, "Two of you barrage the crescent, and someone else help me barrage the other!"

Escapo got off a fine array from his oversized rifle, while Cactus unleashed a full clip from his Desert Eagle hand cannon. Cidel and Ventorin rained down on the crescent. Their shots eventually got through, due to the weakened armor provided by The Mesh's interference. Both drones thudded to the ground.

"Shoot that humanoid while it's offline!" Torcer screamed. "That disruptor only disables it for five minutes!"

Cactus staggered over and unloaded another clip into the humanoid's head. Ventorin cautiously peered up from his partial canopy of stone. "We should take their weapons! We'll need all the firepower we can get!"

"Now why would you want to do that?" came an eerily familiar voice from the sky. They looked up and found a menacing cloud of Z-1 hovering. After an initial freeze from the surprise, they all raised weapons to it, except for Ventorin. He knew their weaponry was no match for it.

Z-1 split into four entities in the shapes of a wild dog, a menacing male face, a bouncing hypercube, and a raging fire. These new shapes surrounded the group.

Escapo swiveled his big cueball-head. "What took you so long to show up?"

"Well, I thought that you all wouldn't stand a chance against some automatons. But it's hard to find good help these days, so I decided to come handle you all by myself."

Escapo grinned. "Bullshit."

Everyone jerked their heads away from Z-1 and to Escapo. Dark clouds rolled quickly with the increasing wind. Thunder and lightning blasted over the horizon.

"You're late to the party because you're not running tip-top. You're weak. All those EMOS over the years have taken a toll on you."

The wild dog leaped at light speed and brought Escapo tumbling to the jagged surface. It's glowing fangs gripped Escapo's neck and gave an electric sizzle. Escapo bellowed loud enough to wake the dead.

The four became one again, a red and black cloud waving casually. "If I were weak, could I have done that?" Z-1 boomed arrogantly.

Cidel stared Z-1 down defiantly and said, "Weak ones commit violence. Does that answer your question?"

Cactus raised the quantum disruptor and fired. It had no visible effect. Z-1 cackled.

Then there was what could not be seen, and was not noticed by Z-1. The disruptor caused an impossibly small "backdoor" into Z-1's systems, and Symphy was there to grab the opportunity. Symphy's face had trance-like focus. Caro stopped pacing and took notice. She wanted to ask Symphy what was happening, but thought better of it. No need to distract. Just be patient. It was a strain to not know. Caro walked to her bedroom, and tried to find solace in the abyss outside her window.

Z-1 froze. Everyone else did the same for a micro-moment. Then it flickered uncontrollably, putting on a blinding display of zealous color. It shot into a twisted tree and shot back into the swirling charcoal sky. It roared like a record played devastatingly slow, then jibbered like an old cassette tape smoking forward and coming unraveled. Finally, Z-1 floated with devastating silence, falling slowly, back and forth, like a sheet of paper dropping through the air, gave a few more slight flickers, and vanished from sight.

Symphy gasped and shuddered. The connection Symphy had had with Z-1 for that brief instant had jolted her own system with unknown forces. Could this be what emotions are like?

The soaked and wind-whipped crew stood on a mound of uncertainty and gawked around in silence for a second. Torcer was the first to speak, "Would one of you geniuses care to tell us what the hell just happened?"

Setarcos and Ventorin gave awestruck shrugs. Escapo showed teeth. "The EMOS."

Cactus said, "We need to move, regardless. We're almost to the rendezvous point."

They carried on in silence. Things stretched and distorted for Cactus as he struggled to cross the finish line. It's funny how the end of a long journey seems to take infinitely longer than all points previous.

The A.I. government grid had received cascading errors due to its connection with the out-of-control Z-1. Nevertheless, two attack ships, one from the north and another from the south, were bearing down quickly on Masher's position. One of those ships had destroyed the original rescue boat shortly before the EMP. The ship that had launched the EMP was on the verge of being captured as well. It was up to Masher. It couldn't do any evasive maneuvers. It was too risky. If it moved, it might not be there to pick up the crew, and they'd be stranded.

Finally, the battered group could see the jagged shores in the distance. Ventorin throbbed with anticipation. It had been over 13 years since he'd been away from Patagonia, and nearly all of that time he'd been held there against his will.

Torcer was filled with uncertainty. What did Cactus intend to do with him? Surely, he would seek vengeance for all the pain Torcer had caused him. Either way, in the hands of his A.I. bosses, or at the mercy of Cactus, his personal prospects didn't look good.

Cidel was suddenly hit with a jolt of uncertainty as well. The prospect of actually surviving this preposterously dangerous mission was now becoming a serious possibility. Ventorin was back, so what would happen to his relationships with Caro and Setarcos?

The wind and rain steadily increased as Masher went out to greet them. "We've got to hurry. There are two attack ships on the way and will be here shortly."

The small boxy ship steadied itself with its nano-stabilizers against the harsh rolls of the waves. It extended a transparent walkway over the tumultuous spaces between it and the arrivals.

Everyone shuffled in with renewed vigor and relief. After boarding and enclosing themselves in the cozy cabin, Masher and The Mesh launched them back towards the open sea.

Cactus approached Masher stealthily. "We need to make a pit stop."

"Now is no time for jokes, Cactus."

"Take me and Torcer to The Moneybit."

Masher viewed Cactus's old ship as it drifted, barely afloat, and badly damaged, just a few kilometers offshore. After seeing this internally, Masher said, "You've got to be crazy. That thing won't last another hour."

"Now," Cactus grumbled.

"That doesn't make any sense, Cactus."

He wheezed and hacked, and then said, "Soon enough, you'll see why we need to do this. Now please, Masher, change course."

Masher sighed and obliged the crazy old man. Moments later, they were side by side with a severely damaged Moneybit. Escapo looked at Masher wild-eyed, "Are you lost, machine? What the hell are we doing here, next to this old wreck?"

A walkway extended from the top of the mostly submerged splinter up to the bow of the bobbing old Moneybit.

Cactus waved his hand cannon at Torcer. "Come on, we're going."

Torcer smirked at the old man's boldness.

Setarcos was puzzled. "What are you doing, Cactus? What's going on?"

Cactus looked at his young friend, the best human friend he'd had in a long time, and smiled with pure contentment. The contentment of someone who feels just right when they find their purpose and carry it to fruition. "See you in the stars, boy."

Cactus and Torcer went up the walkway and almost lost their balance in the wicked and erratic wind. They tumbled clumsily into the old sailboat. Cactus put on a safety harness to guard against going overboard, and gave one to Torcer as well. "You might want to put this on, Torcer! It's gonna be a wild ride!"

Torcer strapped in and kept amused eyes fixed on Cactus as he got the ship ready for its grand finale. He grabbed Cactus by the shoulder and yelled in his ear, "They'll never escape, you know! Even if they get away now, that boy and his father will be hunted for the rest of their lives!"

Cactus struggled to hold the wheel. The boat rolled 90 degrees and sent the two men on their sides, as they gave a death grip to their safety harnesses. Water was up to their ankles already. The hull's damages were slight, but in these conditions, the negative effects were multiplied.

40 knot winds whipped rain in their faces. The sun was starting to set and the gray sky was fading to black.

Cactus staggered to his feet and hugged the mast to brace himself. Suddenly, he felt, and then saw, the humming attack ship bearing down on their position. Torcer looked out helplessly as he splashed around, unable to keep balance. He turned his head to Cactus, who looked at him simultaneously. Their eyes met. Cactus looked ten years younger. He had purpose. Torcer thought for a moment. Why would the attack ship come for them? Why not the others? It didn't make any sense. Then it dawned on him. That damn tracker chip.

Cactus smiled wide. Torcer laughed harder than he had in years. The bulky attack ship steadied itself and towered next to the small, rolling yacht. A motley mix of drones, roller-bots, and semi-autonomous humanoids came along the edges of the hull. Cactus pulled a smoke cannister, threw it, and shot it. This produced a great cloud barrier between the ships. He tossed the disruptor to Torcer.

The old man pulled a couple of molotovs from his backpack. He set up the remaining dynamite in the kitchen below deck, along with the two molotovs. Cactus double fisted his Desert Eagle and a plasma-flux pistol. They waited for the smoke to clear.

They fired relentlessly. When Cactus ran out of lead, he pulled another plasma-flux and went trigger happy on that too. They held off the incoming invaders for a few moments. Just as they were about to be boarded, Cactus scurried down into the relatively dry area of the kitchen, lit a fuse and smiled. Just as a humanoid was grabbing Torcer and picking him up like a rag doll, a fantastic explosion threw the boat and all of its passengers with a fiery blast into the swirling sea-rage around them.

Symphy gasped and put a shaky hand to her finely angled face. While not an emotion, for synths were incapable of having true emotions, it was the closest that Symphy ever had to having one. A more than fifty year relationship with Cactus suddenly gone.

Caro peered around the corner anxiously after hearing Symphy's reaction. "What is it? What happened?"

"I don't know how to explain, so I'll show you," Symphy said with a jagged tone. The final scene of the life of Cactus played out on the holo-projector in front of Caro's harried face. Tears streamed down. She sat next to Symphy and gave a long squeeze of sympathy. Symphy said flatly, "All others are on board with Masher and are making progress."

Caro closed her eyes and melted in relief. Symphy asked if she'd like to speak with Setarcos. Caro nodded and trembled with a weepy smile. Symphy coordinated the communication relay with Masher and soon Caro was face to face with the exhausted group. Setarcos was tossing rivers of tears and could hardly talk. "Cactus....he..."

"I know," Caro said sadly. "I saw. I'm very sorry, Setarcos."

Ventorin threw a consoling arm around his son. Cidel stood back respectfully, not sure how to act in such a uniquely awkward situation.

Masher interrupted, "We're not out of the woods yet. Symphy, we should cut comms until we get farther out."

Communication was cut. The small and powerful vessel maneuvered through the depths with speed and grace. Masher and The Mesh took a macro view of any remaining threats that loomed in their path back to The Pit. Things were looking good. Cactus's ploy had dealt a vicious blow to the nearest pursuers. His single act had bought enough time for the escapees to gain a huge advantage. Masher marveled internally at what Cactus had done. Not only the innovative deception he'd pulled off, but more impressively, the sacrifice. He had literally sacrificed his own life to give them a better chance at escape.

The wounded, meanwhile, took account of the damage and nursed their aches and pains. Escapo lay in a corner, slumped gingerly on his side to try and ease the pressure on his back. Ventorin used a deep-tissue frequency beam from the med kit on board to treat his burns. Cidel and Setarcos sat in exhausted silence, with heated blankets as they slowly sipped steamy drinks. After about a half hour, Masher happily announced that The Mesh estimated their chances of safe arrival to The Pit to be 91 percent. This sent a huge wave of relief through all the human passengers. This allowed them enough peace of mind to grab a few hours of much needed rest. All except for Ventorin. He was too energized by his freedom. He felt a surge of passion as he watched the deep sea life flash by outside his artificial environment. He smiled internally and breathed deeply, with vast contentment at finally being out of captivity.

Chapter 30

"Mom, I can't breathe," Setarcos managed to squeeze out his vocal cords. Caro loosened her iron-grip bear hug a bit. She sighed and cried more tears of joy. She had her son back. Setarcos laughed, "I gotta breathe if I wanna build a space ship, ya know."

She choked and smiled at his wit. She released him and glanced at Ventorin, then at Cidel. They were both standing on the other side of the living room. The two men stood near each other, hands in pockets, uncertain about what to do.

Ventorin wasn't sure if Caro would want him back in her life after all these years. He imagined that she was content with her life with Cidel.

Cidel, on the other hand, still held angst towards Caro. She had deceived him throughout their entire relationship. How could he get past that? Not only that, but now with Ventorin back in the picture, what would Caro want? Would she want to remain with the man she'd been with for the past 12 years, or go back to Setarcos's biological father?

Escapo stood nearby, speechless. He didn't really know why he was still there. He felt like running away. Even though he'd helped rescue Setarcos, he was sure that total forgiveness was completely out of the picture.

Symphy also stood by, with her typically perfect posture. Her normally stoic face, however, had a deep, distant, thoughtfulness about it.

Setarcos and Caro broke free from each other for a moment. He went to Symphy. She went to Escapo.

"Escapo," she said pointedly.

He looked at her with big, sad eyes, like a puppy that was seeking forgiveness. "Yes, Caro."

"Thank you for helping to bring my son back." She continued, "Now get out of my house."

Escapo nodded and forced a smile. Then he looked over to Setarcos, who locked eyes with him, then looked away. Escapo exited in silence, never to be heard from in The Pit again.

Caro turned her attention to Cidel and Ventorin. They glanced around at each other. Ventorin broke the ice. "So Symphy said I could stay at her place until I get things figured out."

"That's very kind of her," Caro said.

Cidel took a deep breath. He could see from the looks on their faces, especially Caro's, that Caro and Ventorin still had a deep love for each other. He made a gut-wrenching decision in the moment. "Don't leave on my account."

Caro and Ventorin looked at him curiously. He continued, "I've decided not to stay in The Pit."

"Cidel," Caro began.

He didn't stop. "No, Caro. It's ok. I'm going to head into the open waters for a while, try to clear my head."

Caro looked at him sadly. "I'm so sorry, Cidel."

"I am too," he said sheepishly. A tear streamed down his cheek. "I won't head out for a couple days. I'll say my good-byes then."

Setarcos was speaking with Symphy. "Symphy, you look different than normal. You almost look sad."

Her lip curled and eyes widened. "Your perceptions serve you well, Setarcos." She paused, then continued, "I don't know how to explain it. My neural pathways somehow grew so accustomed to the presence of Cactus in my life, over so many decades, that now it is as though a small piece of me is missing."

She looked him sharply in the eyes, "Is this what emotion is like?"

Setarcos marveled at his companion. He smiled with wonder, "Sounds pretty close to me."

She looked him up and down. Her facial expression changed. "Well, young Setarcos, we'd better stop standing around."

"Why is that?"

"We've got a space ship to build."

He grinned excitedly and his eyes burst with desire. "The homecoming party is over, huh?"

SeAgora is part three of The Evolution Saga.

The Evolution Saga Timeline

2028 – **James Bong series** begins, bringing the message of truth/true anarchy through moral action, helping people defend themselves against the state, while simultaneously exposing the crimes of the state, All documented online, on various blockchain media platforms, becomes popular.

2029 – B. Light begins to plan and build a secret, voluntary community of anarchists at sea, in an effort to dodge the state completely and attain freedom. Calls it "The C.A. Salt Project"

2030-2053 – **C.A. Salt series.** Development of the "SeAgora".

2045 – Governments learn of "rebels" living undocumented at sea and begin black ops to hunt and destroy them. Part of this operation involves building a vast quantity of A.I. machines.

2053 – The dark occult ruling class begins to have their power usurped by A.I.

2078 – **SeAgora novel** – SeAgorists invent a way to separate dark matter/dark energy in a stable fashion, allowing for speeds many times the speed of light. Land based governments, ruled by A.I., try to steal this information. In the process, the top two A.I. in the hierarchy fight each other and destroy themselves, plunging the ruling hierarchy into disarray. One of those A.I. had become addicted to a synthetic form of emotions for A.I. called "Emos", which played a large role in the ensuing violent chaos and downfall.

2080 – **The Great Agora Space Race Series** – SeaAgorists achieve first successful launch of a SPEED drive, faster than light speed. Land based societies are split into loyalties to different A.I. factions.

2100 – SeAgorists launch into space to begin first human/A.I. settlement.

2578 – **Agora One novel** – The Voluntary Agora is spread across many galaxies. Only moral societies develop the abilities necessary to travel to and settle deep space. Agora One is a planet-sized ship, the first of its kind, able to travel across galaxies within weeks. Back on earth, those who kept the false belief in authority continued to plunge into deeper tyranny and became total slaves to EMO-addicted A.I.

toddborho.com

Made in the USA
Las Vegas, NV
07 January 2026